# Flashback
## To The Mosquito

# Flashback
## To The Mosquito

# Terri L. Powers

**Flashback To The Mosquito**

ISBN (e) 978-0-9915915-0-3
ISBN (sc) 978-0-9915915-1-0
ISBN (hc) 978-0-9915915-2-7

Printed by CreateSpace, An Amazon.com Company
(www.CreateSpace.com/4641541)
Available on Amazon.com and other online stores.

This is a work of fiction. Names, characters, places, and incidents either are the product of the author's imagination or are used fictitiously. Any resemblance to actual persons, living or dead, events, or locales is entirely coincidental. While most of the locations in Flashback to the Mosquito are imaginary, some of the streets and city sites have been unaltered. All persons, police departments, and governmental agencies mentioned in this novel are either fiction or used fictitiously.

Cover design by Dan Stiles at DanArt865@yahoo.com

For Natalie and Marsha, loyal supporters and friends—even though I kill one off in the beginning and the other suffers for it. Thank you for being there.

## Acclaim for Terri Powers' Flashback Series

Book One: Flashback To The Dragon

Powers does a great job of getting you into the mind of the killer, their motives and actions ... Patience is not a virtue I possess, but in this case, it is the only option I have. I will have to wait until I can enter the world of C squared crime solving duo again. ... relax and let Powers take you on a trip. I do not believe you will walk away unsatisfied.

*Capital Area Women's Lifestyle Magazine,*
*Manny Garcia, Account Executive*

... a tightly scripted, character-driven and compelling crime thriller. It's chilling, suspenseful, and in places even breathtaking. The ... opening scene gives the story momentum that propels it all the way through.

*Honest Indie Book Reviews, Gary Henry*

# Table of Contents

**Also by Terri L. Powers**

Flashback To The Dragon

## Acknowledgements

My first novel, Flashback To The Dragon, was a monumental learning experience that was both terrifying and rewarding. When the smoke cleared I thought of all the people who helped me along the way. I'm so grateful to that help and wanted to acknowledge the team that got me through this one.

My many thanks go to a friend and expert on all things mental, Max Baisel. Max, I couldn't have developed my killer as well without your help. Your words kept coming back to me as I put pen to paper. Thank you for being the one person I could get down and dirty with during discussions about psychotic behavior (my family just looks at me horrified).

I want to thank my editor, Theresa Crumpton of Inspirare, LLC, whom I met at A Rally of Writers conference in Lansing, Michigan. Theresa was an inspiration to me and really took ownership over the edit—getting to a place I go, the minds of the characters, and breathing even more life into them.

Dan Stiles is the graphic artist who created the covers for both of my books, as well as the brand for my Flashback Series. A true artist, a creative spirit, and a gentle soul. Thank you my friend.

One of my toughest critics and beta readers is my daughter, Rebecca. Becca reads through a draft picking at every little thing that doesn't seem quite right and catches words or phrases that are out of sync. She started doing this at sixteen when I finished my first novel. Sometimes the subject matter horrifies her—not because of its content, but because she knows it comes out of her mother's head—but she can be brutally honest about what works and what doesn't, and I think she likes to tell me what to do (sometimes).

My mother is one of my biggest supporters and is always there waving the Terri flag at writer gatherings, garage sales, and among her friends. She always finds a way to bring up the fact that *My daughter, Terri, wrote a book. You should read it*. Thanks mom. No matter what, I know you are always there.

Thank you to all my friends and family, and friends of family, who have supported me with words, purchases of my book, and promoting on their Facebook and Twitter pages. It thrills me to see your kindness and encouragement.

Thank you to the city of Seattle. I've loved you from afar. You are on my bucket list of places I want to visit. I love the waterfront locations, Pike's Place Market (I learned about you years ago watching *Go Fish*), and the mystery and beauty of the Pacific northwest.

A final thank you to my husband, Mark. You are always there for me. You always believe in me. And even though the thriller genre is not your cuppa tea, you read my stories and encourage me to continue. If not for you, I may not have stepped off the writing diving board to begin this obsession. I love you.

## Preface

I started the Flashback series one sunny afternoon while sitting on my front porch watching the squirrels watch the birds eat the seeds I'd just put out. I thought of the ability to flash back in time because it's something I've always wanted to do, in fact, it was something I wished I could do on that sunny afternoon to see the neighborhood during the year my house was built, 1898.

The process started in my brain—how do I make a flashback ability relevant in a current murder mystery. I didn't want to write about a cold case. That's when the "how" came to me and the rest of the story followed. I created John Carpenter, a first born child to an older couple who raise their children in a stable and safe environment. John is an accountant with a modest income, nice apartment, a circle of work friends—acquaintances, really, with the only difficulty in his life being his younger sibling, Brandy. John's "bubble" is burst one day on the way to work when a semi runs into his car as it goes through a green light. John is in an induced coma so that his body can repair itself. During that time, a serial killer begins stalking women and Detective Nate Cliffton is anxious to catch him. I pair John and Nate up—one with the cocky attitude and a devil-may-care smile, the other with an ability to flashback and an urgent need to feel relevant.

Location, location, location. Seattle is my city of choice because it is large (population of approximately 627,000), it covers a variety of terrains (Puget Sound waterfront, hills, lakes) and it is located 113 miles south of the U.S. – Canadian border. So I researched maps and websites for almost a year before I began the story.

I write because I have this story to tell about John and I want to get it out there, hopefully to readers who enjoy the story as well. I hope you enjoy reading my books because I enjoy writing them.

# Chapter 1
## *May 4th – 8:15 p.m.*

The evening sun will soon be a memory like the dancing image on the inside of the eyelid after a camera flashes before you can blink. This is my favorite time of day. When the sun touches the water. When the fiery ball softens to merge with the ocean. When work is done, people have gone home, and I am alone to pursue my favorite hobby.

On the bridge of *The Mosquito,* legs apart to balance, I pretend the boat I pilot is mine. And if I wanted, I could sail away into that beautiful sunset. A salty breeze pushes and probes, yet never penetrates my yellow McIntosh. The diesel engines rumble until I pull back on the throttle. The low growl fades. Flip of a finger and muted light surrounds me. The familiar smell of diesel and salt makes up the air.

Slow and confident I move around the forty-one footer. *I could do this in my sleep.* On the starboard side is a cleaning table where tonight's catch is waiting to be cleaned and filleted. I awaken the hose; cold saltwater puts life into the previously lifeless form. It flops around on the metal slab. I twist the nozzle and the feed from the ocean slows to a trickle, then stops. In a leather case, worn to a smooth finish from years of use are my tools arranged side by side, small to large. A fillet knife, a boning knife, and a cleaver—heavy. Perfect. I grip the handle—it fills my palm—lift, aim, and chop off the head. *Kerchunk.* It satisfies me.

The head placed aside for later and the broad blade returned to its original spot—*Time to move on.* Next—the boning knife. Find the spot, insert, and rip upward through the stomach cavity. Entrails bubble and spill—dig, scrape, I toss bare handfuls into the waters below. A powerful thrumming ignites my chest. I rinse the disemboweled cavity and water and bits of flesh spill over the edge of the table and into Puget Sound.

The feeding begins. The underwater running lights catch a fin here, a flash of silver scales there. The social sounds of Humpback whales come on the evening breeze. Listen. *What are they saying with their grunts and snorts and barks?* The melodic tune of the pod and the boat's cradle rock are cooling salve applied directly to my central nervous system. Almost done; one thing left. I reach down for the head, curl my fingers into long blonde hair, bring it up to the metal table and spread my fingers to release it onto the flat surface. *Splunck.* It satisfies me.

She's a beauty. Met her on yesterday's charter-fishing cruise. She was part of the morning group that included her sister and her brother-in-law, her nephews, and an older gentleman and his grandson—not part of her family, but signed on to round out the number of people the boat could accommodate on a four-hour excursion.

She'd confided to me that she was staying in a hotel downtown, rather than in the part-time den, part-time guest room at her sister's place. Flirt. Challenged me to buy her a drink before she left Seattle. I showed up tonight. Easy prey. She'd rather stay and play so she agreed to one before joining her family. Something about the shine of her eyes, the twist of her full lower lip. Pretty girl. Tightness in my belly. I wanted this one. What emotions will play out tonight when she doesn't show up for dinner or join the family at the school play where both boys are performing as Wendy's brothers in Peter Pan; disappointment, anger, fear? It is fun to dream up the different scenarios.

A three-foot-high overturned plastic bucket acts as a make-shift stool. Sitting brings me level with her frozen face. A pale path runs from one green eye to her chin. Did she cry somewhere between drugged at the bar and here? My forefinger traces the path. I touch my tongue to the tip and taste salt mixed with a coppery tang. I like women. They always fall in love with me a little; must be my natural boyish charm. Calm settles over me as I stare into eyes that change from green to icy white. I pick up the filet knife to finish my ritual. *Crunch.* It satisfies me.

*Natalie. Pretty little thing named Natalie.*

Bones pop as I stand and stretch. Fingers caress the blonde tresses, professionally highlighted and now streaked with sticky blood. A casual flip sends her into the water. Blonde hair pools around in a halo and disappears beneath the gentle waves.

I pick up my souvenir from the table and shuffle toward the cabin in search of my hidey-hole under the bunk. I'd come across the loose board while cleaning one afternoon. The space behind it is just big enough for a 7-1/4" by 6-3/4" Admiration cigar box that I purchased at a flea market in Florida. I tuck in my latest treasure alongside the others and close the lid, carefully placing the box back and pulling the board flush.

A yawn forces my jaws open and my eyes to water. *Stay out here and sleep or head back in?* I'll head in. A six o'clock group is scheduled for lingcod fishing. I can sleep a few hours before I need to gas up and collect ice for the coolers. I start the engines and turn on the GPS, even though I know which direction to head, and point toward Seattle's shoreline. With one hand on the wheel, I pull out my cell phone. *Don't text and drive.* Smiling, I flutter my thumb over the key pad to type a quick message and hit send. When the confirmation comes through, *Message Delivered*, I toss the phone into the water.

## Chapter 2
### *May 9ᵗʰ - Noon*

The lunch offer, though a few days early, is the smart move for a Mother's Day gift seeing the look of joy on his mom's face. John Carpenter lifts his glass to propose a toast.

"To the greatest mom in the world, may this lunch smooth over the fact that Nate and I have tickets to the Mariners game and I'll miss your Sunday dinner."

"You tell that Nate that he owes me one." She clicks her tongue to show she means business. An old habit. John cringes inside but maintains his smile. His mom takes another sip and her cheeks redden. "Oh this is good, honey. You'll make sure I get home safely."

He stifles a laugh as he jokes, "I'll make sure I get you home safe and sound, although a slightly inebriated Mrs. Carpenter."

"Mrs. Carpenter?" A soprano echo. A woman stands over their table with a face, while not beautiful in the traditional sense, is lit from within with an expression filled with kindness. Brown eyes framed by long, thick eyelashes do not take attention away from the shadow of a dimple on her right cheek. His heart flutters and he feels as if he's slipped into a vacuum. Silence overwhelms and conversations hush. A tiny scar above her left eye and a slight gap between her front teeth combine for a look of strength and vulnerability, and John decides hers is quite possibly the most interesting face he's ever seen. A conservative navy blue dress comes to just below her knees, but the fabric pulls and clings to her curves in just enough of a suggestion of sensual possibilities beyond the severe cut.

"Susan, how nice to see you." His mom responds releasing John from his trance. He shakes his head. The dream girl smiles in greeting. The dimple deepens. "Susan, this is my son, John. John, this is Susan Bishop who works at the local craft store."

The smile that froze on his lips when he first looked up melts —this is the same woman who was invited to his parent's house for dinner to meet him. He wasn't interested in another blind date arranged by his mother so feigned flu-like symptoms. He reaches out to shake her hand. Susan's grip is firm and warm and strangely pleasant. When their hands part the slight tingle in his fingers leaves him feeling their hands are still entwined.

"So nice to finally meet you," she responds. His guilt adds a slight edge to the way she phrases the greeting, however, he likes her voice. *Silky. Nice.*

"Nice to meet you," he mumbles in reply. "Do you come here often?"

Too late the lame response is out of his mouth, but she smiles. Doesn't dismiss him.

"My father's birthday—" She gestures toward a tall silver-haired man striding toward them. "It's the only time he lets me buy his favorite—veal scaloppini." She ends with a melodic Italian accent. He gulps water from his drinking glass.

Susan introduces the older, male version of herself. Steven Bishop tilts his head and flashes a dimple. John's mom flutters her hands and simpers to his embarrassment. *There will not be another glass of wine in her immediate future.*

6

Father and daughter say goodbye and turn to walk to their table. John attempts to stand and bow, but the opportunity for chivalry is gone. He sits and stares at his plate.

"Nice girl," his mother goads. "I'll bet you wish you came to dinner over a year ago."

John watches her out of the corner of his eye. "You know you're the only woman for me, although for a moment I thought I'd have to pull you off her father."

"I was only being friendly." She looks at him sternly, but can't hold the expression and laughs.

"A lot has happened since that botched dinner date." John pats her hand. "Care for dessert?—Coffee?"

"Oh, I couldn't … I really shouldn't, should I? Well, maybe just a bite of something chocolate and sinful. Don't tell your father."

While they wait for the chocolate mousse, his mom prattles on about her recent bridge club and one of the players, Nancy McCoy, who kept asking about John and how he was doing since the accident. "I think she was prying, trying to find out if you'd grown another nose or something." John lets the words flow into his ears to form a cottony veil over his thoughts. He recalls April of last year and the crash that put him in a coma. Three weeks later he woke up. A week after that he had his first experience. Sitting on the porch of his parent's Victorian home he closed his eyes for a minute to rest. When he opened them he was looking at a 1800s street scene. He remembers blinking back tears that welled when he thought he had either died or gone insane. Shaken by the end of the event, he didn't leave the house for a week. The ability to flashback in time wasn't in his realm of supernatural possibilities. As a kid, he imagined being a superhero with abilities related to strength, speed, or flying. Seeing into the past didn't seem very sexy at all, however, since last year he's learned to turn it to his advantage and take pride in it.

Lately, however, are the headaches—sometimes mild, other times more severe—and niggling doubt creeps its way in that the headaches are not caused by a sinus infection but something more severe and related to the flashbacks. He'll talk to his doctor about the headaches, not the flashbacks, at his next check up in June. He's only told one other person about the strange ability. Their desserts arrive, bringing John back to his mom's announcement that his dad has joined a cribbage league.

"Howard hasn't won any money, but he has such a good time. The league meets once a week, Wednesday night. And your sister has joined a local theatre group." She mashes one bit of information into another and he feels another headache coming on. He is relieved when the check arrives. As he waits for his change, John thinks about Susan Bishop and how to casually find himself in the neighborhood of the craft store.

Chapter 3
*May 10th – 4:00 p.m.*

The *Sea Mistress,* a commercial-fishing vessel hailing from the Seattle area and piloted by Captain Robert Fenton, is plying the waters off the west coast of Whidbey Island. Captain Fenton's plan is to bring in a full load of lingcod, a good-eating bottom fish open for fishing in Puget Sound from May 1st to June 15th. The meat is a cross between true cod and halibut, firm white meat good for fish and chips. The *Sea Mistress* uses a technique of selective fishing, incorporating special equipment. The nets designed to catch targeted species of fish are set for the final haul, and the *Sea Mistress* trolls—one more run for the day.

Bells peal, men shout, and machinery clangs. The last load comes up from the bottom. Steering the net over the deck, one fisherman releases the edges, and the catch tumbles down. With gloves and rubber boots crew members wade in to sort, toss the errant log or tire into one pile, and throw back the unwanted or off-season fish, anything but the lingcod. Halfway through the pile the largest crew member, Sammi, stops and cries out. He rushes starboard, leans over and vomits.

The captain strides to the sick crewman, who points to the deck. Amid the flopping fins and scales, lays a lump of seaweed. He peers closer. It's not all seaweed. Some of its blonde hair. Captain Fenton freezes, a statue staring at a face peering out from under the plant life—his brain trying to tell his body what to do next. A crab scurries out of the open mouth and across the deck. Sammi again leans over the side of the boat only to dry-heave. Captain Fenton places a hand on Sammi's broad back.

"Are you okay now?"

Sammi nods and Captain Fenton asks him to go get a trash bag. He growls at the rest of the crew to finish sorting what was left of the load. When the trash bag arrives, Captain Fenton breathes deep the tang of the water's brine and the wild scent of the sea life flopping on the deck to settle his seafarer's stomach. Then he stoops and gently covers the head with the bag and rolls it up in the plastic and puts it in one of the empty coolers used for cold beverages. Picking up the cooler he nods to his men on the way to the cabin.

As if the woman is merely sleeping and he doesn't want to wake her, he places the container on the floor by a built-in bench. Straightening, he stands with hat in hands and eyes closed for several seconds. Then he jots down the Sea Mistress' current coordinates.

*When we dock, I'll turn over the cooler and its contents to the proper authorities.*

## Chapter 4
### *May 11th – 10:00 a.m.*

"Hey Sweet Cheeks, what's cookin'?" Detective Nate Cliffton fills the doorway at six-foot-three. With an exaggerated lisp and fluttering eyelashes, he directs the question to the man in the empty examination room.

A Seattle PD homicide detective, Nate works out of the West Precinct, which covers the downtown business area, the waterfront, and surrounding districts. Slender, with a faultless sense of style, he avoids taunts about his Hollywood looks by being a serious investigator, a good detective, and never one to complain about covering on the holidays for one of his co-workers, who need to be home with their family. Since he could have his pick of women—single and married, who were clearly in love with him, many in the building questioned why he's not in a relationship or even interested in anyone. The guy before him knows the answer. They hit it off from the start and Tom is the thumb of the list of friends Nate can count on one hand.

"That line works for you? Really? If that's the best you can do, you'll die alone and miserable." Tom Bates raises an eyebrow and goes back to write on the chart clipped to a notepad.

"Hey, I feel good, the sun is out, unusual I know, and for the past couple months no murders, I'm going to a baseball game tomorrow. Why not be in a good mood, except you called me in here on a Saturday." Nate grins at Tom's bowed head.

Bates, a much sought-after expert used by Seattle

PD, is one of the youngest Forensic Medical Examiners in the state. Whenever anything suspicious surfaces, Tom always calls him. Today something suspicious brings Nate down to The Vault, a nickname for the forensic lab in the basement of the same building as Nate's desk.

"I'm not so sure you'll be able to sit around eating donuts and swapping jokes at your desk much longer."

"Well I won't lose my girlish figure then."

"Yes, well I received a call from a coroner over at the Coast Guard facility. Seems a commercial fishing vessel pulled something out of the water besides lingcod and turned it in late in the afternoon. Coast Guard coroner was going to rule it accidental death—"

"Oh no, until—"

"Until she got suspicious about the wounds. Package arrived this morning."

Nate pulls a cotton face mask off the table of linens and joins Tom at the autopsy table.

Tom unfolds the sheet arranged around the small bundle—a severed head. Long hair. A woman. Half her face is damaged. *This isn't going to be easy.*

"Well, that's not much to go on, any other pieces recovered?" A rumble that turns into a burn flares in his stomach. Several thoughts fight for the right to be heard inside his head. How to get this investigation started with so little to go on won.

"This is it." Tom leans toward the table and pokes at the skin tissue.

"Could it have been a boat motor gone wild or Jaws?" There's always hope this did not result from criminal activity.

Tom straightens. "Look here." He points to the neck area. "The incision that separated the head from the body is too clean and straight. It was done with an extremely sharp object."

"Like a boat motor." Nate is grasping, hoping there isn't a sick mind in the shadows waiting to jump out, laugh at him, and leave him with nothing to go on. Nate closes most of his cases. It's something he can depend on, unlike other aspects of his life. He didn't like his chances with this one.

"With the angle I just don't see how probable. The one thing I can definitely rule out, it wasn't Jaws." Tom's voice and laugh are sarcastic. Nate's hand absently rubs circles on his stomach.

"Also, look here." Tom rolls the head slightly so that the damaged side of the face is pointing up. Nate follows Tom's rubber-encased finger. A grisly nub of flesh and bone.

"Her ear is gone." Nate states the obvious. "Could it have been, you know, eaten by fish?"

"It's sliced off a little too cleanly for it to be considered natural or part of a boating accident."

"Just the right ear?"

Tom nods and Nate's brain begins to catalogue past cases in which a piece of body was sliced off.

"Will you be able to tell me anything more? Toxicology? DNA? Anything? Someone must be looking for her. And how long was she in the water before they found her? Will you be able to give me time of death?"

"I'll run the usual tests on the remaining tissue, see if there are any traces of chemicals. No guarantee. I'll put

13

the DNA in our database to see if anything comes up to identify her.

"I can work with Missing Persons," Nate tilts his head to look at her missing features. "It will be hard to match her to any pictures they may have."

"I'll call a forensic sculptor I know. She can reconstruct the face. You'll be able to take a photo, show it around; get an image out to the public to see if anyone is missing her."

"Won't that take a while?" Nate looks up as Tom heads to his desk, facial mask and examination gloves sailing in an arc toward the disposal bin. Two points. Nate follows, standing behind Tom. As the cap slides off the seated man Nate notices there are fewer sandy-colored strands.

"She's competent and will work quickly on a case such as this," Tom assures him. "As far as how long our victim's been in the water, an immersed body will have a wrinkled appearance after one or two hours. For longer periods of time in water, the skin will start to separate. I'll do the best I can, but if I were to guess I'd say she's been in the water between one and fourteen days."

Nate looks back at the forlorn head staring back at him, or rather turned in his direction since the eyeballs no longer reside in their sockets. "Will you or your sculptor person be able to tell the age of our victim?"

"Should be able to get real close."

"Can you get fingerprints off the skin?"

"I'll run the head through the vapor; see what I find before starting any of the other tests."

"Was Harbor Patrol involved?" Nate wonders

aloud, pondering the jurisdictional red tape.

"I work directly with you. I'll let you work it out between the Coast Guard and Harbor Patrol."

"Ok, let me know as soon as you know anything. Hey, how are Jackie and Michele?"

"Doing well. Shelly's been asking when her uncle Nate is coming for a visit, and Jackie hinted at a date night. You up for a night of babysitting next week?"

"Count me in daddy-o. I'm headed to Missing Persons." Nate's shoulders slouch forward and he points the fingers of his right hand down gangsta-style, "Holla back at me later, dawg."

Tom rolls his eyes and turns back to the computer, but before Nate makes it through the door he hears the man's final words.

"This one didn't come from the streets. I'm sure her death was anything but accidental."

## Chapter 5
*May 13th – 5:30 p.m.*

John waited only three days before calling Susan. She seemed friendly enough over the phone—reserved, but friendly—and had agreed to a meeting. John smoothes an unruly lock of hair and checks his watch for the fourth time in ten minutes. He inhales deeply and exhales, blowing air through his pursed lips. No headache today has him feeling optimistic. The fact that he is still sitting here after the appointed time of their meeting trumps optimism.

The woman seems to bring out feelings unlike any other. Embarrassment because he passed on meeting her a year ago. Confusion because when he thought of her it was as if he's missed a few meals and is hungry for something wholesome, yet spicy.

Seated at a two-top facing the entrance of a small bar-and-grill near Susan's work, he nervously plays with his watch and stares at the door. John sees a woman with the same hair color walk past the plate glass window and keep walking past the front door. *Sigh.* He relaxes back in his chair and again looks at his watch. The second hand has only moved a fraction.

The cell phone vibration makes him jump in his chair. A text. Taking it out of his pocket he squints at the display.

*Can't make our date, a lady at work has the flu and I'm covering her shift. Maybe another time?*

Disappointment. That missed dinner last April flickers around the back of his mind like a moth trying to run itself into a flame. A part of John can't help but think this cancellation is payback. Well, he'll have to keep trying. Come out of his relationship shell and be a little more insistent. Walk up to her at the craft store and demand she go out with him. But not tonight. He motions to his waiter for his bill and scurries back under the safety of his shell.

# Chapter 6
## *May 14<sup>th</sup> – 11:00 a.m.*

The unidentified head is now the center of an open homicide with Nate officially assigned to be the lead investigator. Tom estimated time of death within a seven-day window from the time the victim was found. DNA obtained from the analysis of tissue was run through CODIS on an expedited order, but had come up negative. Nate wants to find more pieces of his Jane Doe. Tom called in Dr. Rebecca Giles, a forensic sculptor, who began work immediately to recreate the woman's features using clay, scalpels, and artist tools to provide an approximate image of what the mystery woman might have looked like prior to death. Dr. Giles had already measured bone density and wear on facial ligaments and teeth and reported to Tom that her educated guess on the age of the victim is early thirties. She hoped to have a bust available for photographing by early June. Nate is hoping its sooner.

After talking to his Lieutenant, the first thing he did was contact the U.S. Coast Guard liaison, Special Agent Lance Lott of the agency's Investigative Service division, to schedule a search-and-retrieval of the area where the commercial fishing vessel pulled in the body part. He took sadistic pleasure with Lott's name when he called yesterday to set up today's operation by asking if the SA had learned from King Arthur that the commoners in Seattle PD would be contacting him. Sometimes it's the little things that get him through each day.

*1:00 p.m.*

The wind musses Nate's hair as the ship cruises to the search location. He enjoys the tangy scent of salt water and the fishy smell on the breeze—pleasant change from the usual scents he encounters during the course of an investigation. The rain cleared around noon, but threatening, fat, gray clouds remain.

Nate is along to observe only and has no intention of ruining this boat trip with a dive into the water once they reach their destination. Living in Seattle for the past fourteen years, he knows Puget Sound and the surrounding rivers and lakes are not something he wants to swim in, let alone dive one-hundred-fifty feet with rough waters and frigid temperatures most of the year.

*Give me a heated pool any time.*

Nate watches Tom Bates in an animated discussion with the Coast Guard and Police Department technicians regarding the Mariner's chances this season. Nate starts a solitary march across the deck. If in the four-hour time slot they come up empty this murder may end up in the cold-case files until something surfaces, literally and figuratively, at some time in the future. He hates when that happens.

The engines shift, the boat slows, and waves that were following quickly catch up to gently lift the vessel. Metal clangs as the anchors drop near Whidbey Island, north of Port Townsend in the area of the Admiralty Inlet.

"Good luck Special Agent Lott," Nate calls out as he watches the SA prepare to go into the water with the rest of the Coast Guard unit. Lott tips the face plate on his gear as a way of saluting and penguin-shuffles toward the side of the boat.

## 2:20 p.m.

One-hour-and-twenty minutes filled with more pacing and chatting with Tom gets interrupted by a commotion at the side of the cutter. A basket rig rises out of the water with two bundles folded in plastic and hooked to the metal frame. Tom and the two agency technicians gather to inspect the contents, taking pictures, but otherwise not touching. Nate watches over their shoulders as they work. He spies a hand, partially stripped of flesh with the nails short and trim. It's a disturbing gray and doesn't look real as it lay curled in the basket. Beside the hand (and more disturbing) is a skull.

Lott is still down there, searching; and another half hour passes before he and the team come up with the last haul of the day, a foot, another hand, and what looks like pieces of bone encrusted with shells. The severed limbs that still contain some tissue vary in color. There's no way to tell how many victims they have found today; only testing will tell for sure. All of the parts will go with Tom to the morgue at the Medical Examiner's Office.

The skull is what disturbs Nate most because it points to the possibility that these killings have gone on for a while; that the woman's head the commercial-fishing crew stumbled upon is one of a whole line of victims.

The officers prepare to return home. Tom and the CSI technicians blow off steam, joking about finding Davy

Jones' locker, or the dumping ground of Hannibal Lecter, anything to cast off the morbid shroud that fell over everyone when the basket rose. Lott sits wrapped in a large blanket. Nate looks over at him. Knows he should talk to him. Decides to focus on the skull.

"Looks like a killer that's been in the business for a while."

"So it would appear. It was a little eerie down there." Lott's voice sounds hollow, pulling Nate in. Nate grimaces, not wanting to get any closer so he pushes away with humor.

"Well, SA Lott, I'd say it's been a successful day for the good guys. Time to get home to Guinevere."

Lott leans close to Nate so that only he hears his next words. "I'm more of a get home to King Arthur kind of guy."

Nate smirks and looks sideways at Lott who smiles back at him, winks and stands to go to the locker area to remove his gear.

## Chapter 7
*May 15, 2013 – 4:45 a.m.*

The sun is about an hour away from making an appearance. The cabin is dark and still, with only the cries of sea gulls and the gentle slap of water against the hull to break the silence. I lie awake in a tangle of blankets. Stare at the wall. Watch the black melt to gray on its way to Technicolor. The air in the cabin is stuffy with the smell of unwashed linens, and the musky wetness from mold and mildew that seeps into every nook and cranny. It comforts me.

Afternoon charter today, so I'm in no hurry to get out into the fresh air to start my day. The high-pitched cell phone chirp draws my attention to the built-in table where the phone, my wallet, and the boat keys are piled. The sound announces that I have a text message. I reach for the phone.

*Caught a beauty last night. Had her 4 dinner. I'm ahead of U. Happy hunting.*

The words bring a mixture of irritation and jealousy. The idea of being lazy ruined, I delete the message and throw off the thin blanket to pull on some jeans and a t-shirt.

# Chapter 8
## *May 17th – 6:30 p.m.*

Crystal Knapp and her boyfriend Chuck Connors enjoy the Friday atmosphere at a quaint bar on the waterfront a short distance from their hotel. From Spokane, they were in Seattle for a few days to celebrate the one-year anniversary of their first date by doing something they enjoy, meet new people and coax free drinks out of strangers. Tonight's dinner at a local restaurant that caters to the charter-fishing crowd was the lingcod they caught that afternoon. For a reasonable price the restaurant cooks the fillets any way the customer wishes: baked, fried, or grilled, and serves it with a tossed salad and bread.

After dinner the couple wanders around a bit and ends up at a place where the crowd is lively and the bartender is friendly and keeps their drinks flowing. Crystal feels no pain when she starts an impromptu dance beside her bar stool and bumps into someone behind her.

"I'm so sorry," she begins. She turns to look into a familiar face with strange and intense eyes. "Hey, aren't you the guy from the boat?"

The eyes do not share in the warmth of his smile. He offers to buy them both a drink. Her face lights up at the offer, and she elbows Chuck. Her boyfriend turns slightly and tips his draft toward the boat guy as a way of saying *hello*.

"What was your name?" Crystal frowns slightly, trying to remember.

"You can call me *the boat guy*." He turns to go in pursuit of their adult beverages. Ten-minutes later the mugs are placed in front of Crystal and Chuck. Thirty-minutes later Crystal swoons on her bar stool. Balancing herself she turns to Chuck to let him know it's time for her to leave.

"My car's not too far from here, if you'd like I can drive you back to your hotel." Their drink benefactor helps clear a path through the crowd for them.

"No, we're fine, we walked from the hotel. It's only a few blocks," Chuck says seconds before Crystal collapses onto the sidewalk. "Mebbee I'll take you up on that offer."

Chuck manages to grab one of Crystal's arms and, with the help of the boat guy, lurches toward the parking lot. Beside a non-descript brown car, Chuck can no longer function and lets go of Crystal.

"Whoa, guess that last beer was one too many," Chuck mumbles and slips to his knees.


### 9:00 p.m.

I start with Chuck. Clean. Gut. Feed the fish. The routine a rhythm to be enjoyed. Unfortunately before Crystal meets the same fate I see lights from a boat. It doesn't appear to be fishing vessel, and it's headed in my direction. I can't finish the ritual, but that doesn't mean I deny myself a memento of this evening. I smooth back hair and lift the cup-shaped ear away from the side of her head and take my trophy. Then I pitch her—fully clothed—into the water. *Dammit! This isn't how my evening is supposed to go.* I slam the boat into gear, and speed well south of the approaching lights.

**11:00 p.m.**

*Way ahead of you now, buddy. Got 2 4 the price of 1 this weekend.* I attach a photo. With black cotton cloth as background, the two pink objects really show up.

## Chapter 9
### *May 19th - 3:00 p.m.*

Mom's Sunday dinner is excellent per usual. Nate is late, coming through the door with a stream of reasons all related to some new murder case. John's invite to Susan— another attempt to get together—failed because she had a work function, so John avoids his mom's inquiries about his social life. After dinner he feels lethargic and needs to get moving so he volunteers to help Brandy in the kitchen while Nate, his mom, and dad go to the living room to relax a bit before they all sit down to a game of Uno. He's careful as he places the last of the glassware on a counter near his sister who is up to her elbows in suds.

"Why do you wash the dishes before putting them in an appliance designed to wash them?"

No answer, just the downturn of her lips. John searches for a dishcloth to use on the table. The low hum of conversation from the other room breaks into louder sounds of laughter.

"Something must have got 'em going," John murmurs. This brings Brandy out of her self-induced silence.

"So big brother, think you could hook Nate and me up for a date? I keep hinting to him that he should take me out, but I think he's scared you'll beat him up. Why don't you ask him to call me; he'd be interested in a date with me, right?"

He dreaded this day would come. Nate's a good looking guy. Ever since Brandy met him, she's hinted and John would pretend he didn't hear. Now it's out in the open with nowhere to run. He avoids her stare by keeping his eyes on the dishcloth, holding it under the running faucet. The cloth is soaked. Nowhere to run. Finally he responds. "Brandy, you're not his type."

"What do you mean I'm not his type? What is his type?" She stands with one hand in the dishwater and one hand propped on her hip. Just like mom.

"Well," John jerks away as a soapy finger rises to point at him. Suds drip onto the linoleum. "His type has blonde hair, blue eyes—"

"Well, I've got blonde hair and blue eyes, well more violet, but they look blue most of the time. You just don't want me to date a friend of yours; tell me that's not the truth of it."

"Ok, let's see, blonde hair, blue eyes ..." He meets Brandy's accusatory violet, not blue, eyes and feels a tug of brotherly concern. "Oh, yeah, and a penis."

He watches the emotions parade across her face ending with suspicion as her lips form an O and clamp shut.

"You better not be pulling my leg about Nate. That would be really mean and totally un-brotherly."

"Bran, I'm not. Nate's a great guy, and I really respect him. He's my friend. But he can't be your boyfriend, even though I think that in itself would be really weird, because he's gay. Not that there's anything wrong with that." John repeats the famous quote from an old sitcom, but as he says it he can't remember the name of the show.

"What a shame," Brandy groans and returns both hands to the water. "He seemed perfect for me."

"Wait, you meet him a few times, and you think

he's perfect. Your standards have simplified." John shakes his head. This isn't the princess on the pea he was used to fighting with.

"Well he saved your life, he gets along with mom and pop, he passed me the potatoes first tonight. And he has those beautiful blue eyes, classy clothes, perfectly styled hair, and he knows so much about the Kardashians, and—" *Argh*, how could I not see he's gay." Brandy sighs.

"Well, if it's any consolation, I think he's broken up with the guy I just mentioned."

"Nope, I want him to be happy. Maybe he and I can just be best buddies, we can shop together, give each other pedicures, and we can do sleepovers ..."

He freezes, unsure of how to respond until Brandy's laughter bubbles. He wrings the dishcloth and turns to go to the dining room. One step is all he manages before the room tilts, his vision blurs, and he can't find his balance. Thudding against the edge of the countertop, Brandy stops laughing. One, two, three ... counting calms him.

"Are you okay?"

Hand pressed against the tile, fingers splayed, he's afraid to let go of the kitchen counter. He brings his free hand up to massage his temple, the washcloth temporarily forgotten on the linoleum floor.

"Just a little dizzy." Slowly he straightens and turns to look at Brandy intending to give her a reassuring smile, but the smile turns into a grimace.

"John, what the hell is wrong with you? I'll call dad—"

"Fuck! NO! Just be quiet."

"You're dizzy and you need help." She keeps

28

placing her hands on both sides of her mouth like she is holding in a moan.

"I'm fine, it's passing." Face red. Mouth in a straight line. He grits his teeth and straightens, leaving the dishcloth on the floor.

"Has this ever happened before?" Her voice up an octave she holds both arms out like that will stop him from falling at her feet. Then wrapping her arms around his waist, she helps him to a chair at the dinette table tucked into a corner of the bright yellow kitchen. He sinks down into the cushioned chair. Her tone puts John on edge and he clenches his teeth, debating telling her anything at all.

"It's just a headache. I think I'm having allergy problems."

"I heard on the news that allergy sufferers didn't have anything to worry about this season because the pollen threat is low."

He didn't like her probing, so he says the one thing he knows will bother her.

"OK mom, stop worrying."

"John, I'm serious. If you don't tell me I'm going to get loud, and then Mom will come running in, followed by Dad or Nate—probably Nate because he's younger with that smoking' hot body and might be more curious than dad; dad would just want to sit—"

"Bran, I'm going in for my CAT scan next month. I'll mention the headaches then. So don't worry."

"I'm coming with you."

He knows he's not going to win this battle, and a part of him is glad she will be there. His family's concern for his well-being, while stifling at times, is heart-warming.

"And you can buy me lunch." She's regained her composure. The fluttery hands are settled. He meets the sly expression in her eyes.

"What? Why should I buy you lunch? I just bought you lunch last week."

"You will want to repay me for covering up tonight and pretending none of this happened."

"Ok, Bran, it's a deal. Now, let's finish up here and get out there before Nate and his smoking' hot body rushes in here to see what's keeping us."

# Chapter 10
## *May 20ᵗʰ – 4:00 p.m.*

The nine days since Nate first saw the head blur. Building a case with little information is a recipe for failure. Last night he met with SA Lott after work to discuss the investigation, but no actual discussion occurred and he had ended up at Lott's apartment, no further along on the mystery than when he'd started, but the benefits of sleeping with SA Lott were rewarding, and gone was the pent-up frustration.

He sits at his desk, comparing notes from the stack of Missing Person files to his own. Tom's toxicology report and DNA results of all the limbs recovered on last week's dive is in a coffee-stained manila folder with the words TO DO followed by a checklist of suggestions that he doubted he could or should ever use. Some smartass had scratched out the NEVER suggestion at the bottom of the list and replaced it with NO WAY IN HELL. The folder is open. Thorazine, an antipsychotic drug used to treat bipolar disorder, anxiety, or aggression was found in the tissue of their Jane Doe, so the question is: was it her medication or something that was used to disable her prior to death? His cell phone chirps dragging him away from a report he's read seven times this morning.

"Hey John,"

"Hey Nate. What are you doing tonight? Want to grab a burger and a beer?"

"How 'bout at the Pub."


*6:00 p.m.*

The Pub is short for Bridge Street Pub and Grill, their favorite hangout and home to some of the best burger combinations in the area—bleu cheese and maple bacon, jalapenos and pineapple, or prosciutto and fried egg. John arrives first and sits at the bar. He only has to sit by himself a few minutes.

"I ordered you a draft," John says.

"Bless you, my son." Nate grabs a barstool and sits. "What's up? I thought you'd be bored with me. You saw me yesterday and now today. Don't want the honeymoon to end?"

John's knee jumps around, a nervous tic. "How's the case going?"

Nate waits until after they order to answer.

"I'm still waiting. Forensic sculptor's doing her thing. I got nada."

John's eyebrows come together in a scowl. "I thought maybe I could help, but if you've got nothing, then you got nothing."

"Why so down, Bubba?" Nate asks.

"Aw, I'm not. Not down really," John shrugs. "I just wish I could help. It makes me feel good to help. Who knows how long I'll have this ability."

"Whoa, what do you mean?"

"Don't get me wrong. It's not like you couldn't catch bad guys without me."

"No, not that, what do you mean you don't know how long. Are you losing the flashbacks?"

"No, no, no, at least, not yet."

"You had me worried. You and your flashbacks

32

make my life so much easier. If I could use you now, you know I would." Nate rewards John with a pat on the shoulder.

"Aw, forget it." John ducks his head, like a turtle trying to get out of the sun.

"That's not the only reason I love you," Nate teases. "And if you ask me, you *are* important. Your purpose is to make me laugh and forget about the streets. Mission accomplished."

"It's a full-time job, too. You're not easy—"

Nate's cell phone rings, and he holds a finger up to stop John. Looking at the screen, he sees its work and takes the call.

"Cliffton. I'll meet you there."

John cocks an eyebrow at him.

"Body just floated up on shore at Mutiny Bay."

"Over on Whidbey?" John shivers. He hates the water.

Nate nods and throws a twenty on the table. "I've got to go catch a boat."

"Ok, remember, if you ever need anything. Anything that is except a flashback over the water. Or in a boat. Or near the water."

Nate laughs. He understands about the water. Then he pounds his fist over his heart twice and throws John the peace sign with two fingers. John returns the familiar gesture.


*7:30 p.m.*

33

Nate arrives at the marina after a drive across town that broke records as far as speed and time. He and Lance take a Harbor Patrol boat to Whidbey Island. An Island County Sheriff's Deputy meets them at Mutiny Bay and races the short distance from the dock to the location of the body that swept up onto a sandy beach at a time when residents and visitors were having their pre-dinner walk. Fully clothed, barefoot, hair disheveled and covering a face lifted toward the sky. The neck at an impossible angle.

Nate looks around noting the wooden posts rising above the water where a dock once stood and cottages in a line about fifty-yards away from shore. His perusal ends at the area beyond the yellow-caution tape, where curious onlookers are gathering. The crime-scene technician snaps photos.

Nate gestures with a head nod toward the crowd. "Take a photo of the people."

Lance joins Nate. Nate reaches over and buttons the top two of Lance's London Fog overcoat. "Can't have you catching cold."

Lance chuckles, finishing the job, and glances over toward the crowd. "I can start questioning them, see if anyone saw anything."

Nate nods, and Lance sloughs through the sand. Nate watches him walk away. Tom Bates gets out of a sheriff's car and heads his way, showing his ID to the officer guarding the area.

"Another Jane Doe?" Tom asks as he nears Nate.

"Not sure, I'm waiting to get in there."

The crime technicians set up lights around the victim to stave off the oncoming night and begin taking photos of the body. Nate kneels, balancing over the body. With gloved hands he gently pushes the hair covering the victim's face, smoothing it away from the forehead and cheeks, pulling it from under the neck, so that features are revealed. Nate gets the attention of the technician taking photos and points down at her face. Nate carefully rolls the head to the left and asks the technician to take a picture to note the missing ear on the right side. He and Tom share a knowing glance. Nate searches the pockets in soggy jeans hoping for some identification. There's nothing in her jeans pocket or her shirt pocket. Nate stands, knees popping.

"At least this one is fairly whole. Make it easier to identify. Sheriff's office called our office when the deputy saw the mutilation, quick thinking on their part. Have a look; I'm going to talk to the two guys that found her."

Nate walked up to the sheriff, who escorted him to the scene.

"Maybe you guys will help us out with interviewing any fishermen, who were known to be out last night. Maybe they saw something."

The sheriff indicates he'll get right on it. Nate turns back to look at the body Tom is preparing for transport.

*What changed the mystery killer's ritual?*

## Chapter 11
*May 22ⁿᵈ - 12:30 p.m.*

Nate stares at a photo of a woman—classically good-looking with blonde hair and hazel eyes. The eye color was Dr. Giles' best guess. She completed the sculpture of the first victim yesterday, way ahead of schedule. Dr. Giles intimated that it felt as if the head spoke to her through her fingertips, and she worked until midnight most nights. Yesterday she finished at four in the morning, showered, had breakfast, packaged the sculpture, and presented it to Tom when his office opened at eight. She would now work on the skull retrieved during the dive on the 14th, but only after a twenty-four-hour nap.

Yesterday Nate took photographs of the sculpture to his contacts at two local news stations and a Seattle newspaper. The television stations ran a clip throughout the day, and sent the story to their radio affiliates. An article hit the afternoon papers and again this morning. Come forward helpful someone. Someone who knows her. Someone who will talk to him. Someone with a clue. He feels like he's in a poker game watching the dealer flip the cards toward him. Snatch the new cards into his hands, turn them over one by one, only to be the wrong cards; the right card just out of reach, still in the pile. He waits. Nerves—*ping, pling, ding*—stretch to their limit.

Tom said he'd have something this afternoon for the body on the beach so when the phone rings, Nate ignores the display and quickly reaches across his desk for the receiver, brings it to his mouth, and snaps into the mouthpiece, "Hey Tom."

"H—hello, are you the detective on the missing-woman case?" The voice is low, almost a whisper. The sound like glass in the act of cracking. Like a windshield with a chip that slowly inches its way across the entire surface.

Nate hesitates, his brain scrambles to change gears when it's not Tom's baritone that he hears. "Ma'am, how can I help you?"

"I have an awful feeling ..." Jagged breathing.

Nate's heart accelerates. He grabs a pen and prompts the woman to continue. "Ma'am is there something you wish to tell me?"

A soft moan floats through the phone. It chills with its hopelessness. The icy notes come through the phone into his ear and settle in his chest. The freeze hollows out his heart. Three words float through the air.

"It's my sister."


## 1:30 p.m.

Marsha Jones and her husband, David, are sitting in the conference room Nate reserved in order to talk to them in private. Marsha begins the interview with the unnecessary detail that she tried, too late, to turn off the television so that the boys wouldn't see, but they looked up from their cereal this morning in time to wonder what Aunt Natalie was doing on TV. The kids were staying with friends after school.

"I'm so sorry for your loss." Nate is conditioned to say this phrase every time he meets with a victim's family, but unlike some of his fellow officers, Nate really is sorry and feels their pain, having himself a family torn. "Can you tell me a little about your sister's time in Seattle?"

"She didn't stay with us. If she had, she might still be alive today." David reaches over for Marsha's hand and squeezes.

"She was staying at the Andra Hotel. Said she didn't want to be in the way. I told her she wouldn't be. We had plenty of room, but she insisted. Said she wanted to get the flavor of the city." Marsha starts rocking back and forth in the chair, holding herself with her free hand. Nate takes down the name of the hotel and nods to encourage Marsha to continue.

"She did the usual tourist activities, alone or with us. The last day, the last time we saw her; it was the day we went on a charter boat for some fishing. We got back from the charter, had lunch and parted." She folds over on herself as if this last sentence dried her out and her shell can no longer support the Marsha she used to be. David places a hand on the middle of her back and starts massaging, worry etches his face. He picks up the conversation.

"Natalie was supposed to come for fish dinner the next night. We were fixing what we caught and then going to the boys' school play. She never showed."

Marsha recovers and sits back in the chair, wiping her eyes with a tissue. She remains quiet.

Nate continues to address David. "What time would this have been?"

"Seven. The play started at nine, but the boys were supposed to be there an hour early, so we were going to head over to the school at quarter-to-eight."

"When she didn't show, did you call?"

"Of course." Irritated. Clipped. Marsha sounds as if I have just insulted her. "I called her cell phone, but she didn't answer so I left a message. At seven-thirty she still hadn't shown up. I called again. Then I called the hotel and had them ring her room. When it looked like she wasn't coming, we all left."

"You were worried?" Nate keeps his posture open, encouraging responses. Marsha looks at David. *Something's going on here. The look means I'm about to hear something good.*

"We were worried, of course. But then around eight, I received a text from her. She's done this before."

"What did the text say?"

"She met someone who was interesting and funny and was headed to Portland for the rest of her stay."

He can feel his scalp pinging and Nate leans forward in his chair. "Do you still have it?"

Marsha reaches into her purse for her phone and passes it to him.

He punches the message labeled *Natalie* and reads the display. A thought builds in his head. Could the message be a diversion—a taunt? "Does this sound like her? I mean, no apology for skipping out on the play, is the phrasing like her?" *No slam bam thank you ma'am.* Marsha's blank look answers. She reaches for the phone to reread the message, brows knitted.

"I don't know. I didn't think of that. Oh God, do you think …"

Nate cuts her off with a shake of his head. "I don't

know what happened. Let's get back to the facts. You saw Natalie up until the afternoon of the fishing trip. You did not have contact with her or see her after that time. I'm assuming she must have had transportation while in town."

Both of them nod and Marsha fills in the details. "She rented a car from Seattle Sights Rent-A-Car."

Nate wrote this in his tablet. Pieces of the puzzle. "What prompted you to file a missing persons report if, as you said, she's done something like this before?"

"When I first got the text, I assumed it was Natalie being Natalie. Always whatever she wants no matter who gets hurt. So, naturally, I was mad. But then the hotel called a few days later." Marsha's shoulders slumped as if she were caving in.

David leaned toward Nate. "We thought maybe she forgot to check out or left a balance. They did ask that we pay the balance, but also wanted us to pick up her belongings."

"And the hotel knew to call you because ...?" Nate looks at them from under his eyebrows.

"They had our number. I made the reservation." Marsha responds. She seems stiff. Guilty. Nate shrugs it off as a side effect of her grief. He glances down at the picture the Joneses brought in of a vibrant woman with flashing green eyes. The similarities are there, except for Dr. Giles' eye color choice.

Nate thanks them and gets their contact information. Marsha provides a list of places they visited with Natalie and a list of her friends. Nate notices a nervous twitch to her hands as she writes the names on the paper he provided. He promises quick resolution to their legal claim of the body. The Joneses walk out of the office and toward the elevator, holding onto each other. The last hour aged them. Nate would like to believe Natalie sent the text. That she was having a great time down in Portland. Unfortunately, Natalie's head is shocking evidence to the contrary and the text message a chilly epitaph.

### 3:00 p.m.

The mirrors in the office's restroom reflect John in bad florescent lighting. His twin tips a plastic sixteen-ounce bottle of water. More aspirin. *Another headache; this makes three days in a row.* The face is haggard, with faint blue smudges under the eyes.

In twenty-one days he's scheduled for his final CAT scan, or computerized axial tomography, the required follow-up to his head trauma. The last CAT scan was in October of last year and came back clean, but right after the clean bill of health the headaches started.

His cell phone rings, interrupting the inspection. The name that pops up on the screen is Nate Cliffton.

"Hello buddy, what's up?"

### 5:15 p.m.

John walks from his office to their usual hangout, enjoying the golden warmth from the sky as it hits the top of his head. His mind wanders. He thinks about the headaches. He thinks about the flashbacks. He thinks about the first time he met Nate. He felt like a suspect, sitting in a hard wooden chair answering questions and supplying his alibi even though he'd only come to the police department to report a possible murder. In the end, his flashbacks caught the serial killer, something he's still proud of.

The flashbacks aren't always convenient. Last week, in fact, while shopping in Pioneer Square, the sky blackened, the air filled with the acrid smell of burnt wood and singed hair, and he found himself surrounded by burning buildings, screaming people, and rampaging livestock. He sweated it out for the first few seconds of the flashback until he realized he was viewing the terrible fire that swept through the area back in 1889. John shakes his head when he remembers the chaos. Soon he is at the front door of his destination. He barely slows as he passes through the entrance. When his eyes adjust to the lighting, he sees Nate waving him over to the bar.

"I ordered you a Coke."

"Thanks, man." John sits and pulls closer to the polished wood counter and meets Nate's icy blue eyes. "What?"

"You look like Hell."

"Couldn't be better."

"Are we going to lie to each other today? Next time, wear a sign so I remember to bring my own lies to the party."

"Geesh can't get away with anything with a detective." John mumbles into his chest.

Nate flashes his trademark smile and adjusts his shoulders in a jacket that would cost two of John's paychecks. "Just part of my charm."

"I had a headache this—"

"You called a doctor."

A statement. John felt his face flush. "No, I've—"

"Why not?"

"My routine check-up is next month—"

"Do I need to march you in myself?"

"You're not marching me in anywhere."

"You never know, you could like it." Nate smirks at him sideways.

"There you go again, always trying to bring me over to the dark side."

"It's not dark. It's mood lighting."

John rolls his eyes and Nate bumps a shoulder against his. "I'm just kidding, Bubba. So next month. Anything to worry about?"

"I plan to tell them all about the headaches."

"Yeah, but you shouldn't wait."

"I promise, next headache I have I'll go to emergency. Do not pass go. Do not collect two-hundred dollars. Come on. Tell me why you called."

"You need to take care of yourself. You're a hot little commodity." Nate winks before launching into his request. "It's the case I'm working on—"

"The unknown woman?"

"Yeah, we know who she is now."

"I saw something on the news. So someone must have come forward."

"Yeah, her family. I'm hoping you'll have a helpful memory at the Andra Hotel where she stayed. You in?"

John slaps the bar with both palms. "Sure, when?"

Nate's eyes glint like a kid set to con somebody.

"Can you clear your calendar for this evening?"

*6:30 p.m.*

They arrive at the Andra Hotel, a stately 1926-nine-story in the Belltown district. Over the years, the interior has undergone modifications to maintain its elegant and comfortable reputation. John and Nate walk into the lobby. To the right, is a fireplace in front of a cozy arrangement of chairs and loveseats, to the left is a bar leading to a restaurant. In the center of the lobby is a pond filled with water and surrounded by stones that reflect the colors of the interior of the hotel. A bright flash breaks the surface— Goldfish in search of food. The atmosphere of the hotel is opulent and whispers: *get ready to be pampered and thoroughly rested, dahlink.*

John follows Nate to the check-in counter where the detective shows his badge to the hotel manager and presents his warrant. The manager's face fills with disdain, as if Nate just handed him a moldy rat. "Detective." A cool response. Nose pointed toward the chandelier overhead.

Nate returns his badge to his jacket pocket as if removing it from the little man's sight will wipe the pinched look off his face. "I'd like to get into room 626."

"I'm sorry, that room is booked." The manager didn't even glance at the registration in front of him.

"I understand that this may not be a good time—"

"It's never a good time. Is there a surface or cupboard you neglected to mar?"

Nate's voice continues in a soothing tone as he

44

turns to acknowledge John. "The consultant and I will only be thirty minutes."

"Housekeeping took a full day to undo the damage the last time you folks were here."

"Look. Help me out. I've got a girl, one that stayed in your hotel, and now she's dead. Her family. Nice people, live over near Bellevue. I'd like to do right by them."

John tenses. He watches the staring match between both men. Seconds tick, tick, tick away.

"Very well." the manager breaks down first and John subconsciously feels Nate celebrate when the detective stands taller and leans forward over the shorter man behind the registration counter.

Ten minutes later John and Nate are in an elevator headed for the sixth floor. Room 626 wears an expectant mantle as if waiting for a knock on the door and a maid to appear with more towels. John suspects it is because the people staying in the room recently vacated and were waiting to get back in, sitting in the restaurant on the Andra's dime. He slowly walks around the room, as if dancing a freestyle waltz, trying to put himself in the right frame of mind. Waiting to be sucked into the past. He imagines Natalie, her image from the photo Nate showed him earlier floating in his mind. *She walks over to the window, brushes the curtains aside to see the view from this floor.* He's overlooking 4th Avenue. The traffic rolling smoothly past. Turn, let the drapes fall. *She walks toward the bathroom.* He flicks a switch and light spills from the vanity.

Thirty minutes pass before Nate, tapping his toe and fidgeting asks, "Anything?"

45

John shakes his head.

"Okay, shall we leave?"

John nods and Nate leads the way into the hall.

"This place is really beautiful," John notices the crown molding in the hallway.

"Let's check out the lobby and the street in front of the entrance," Nate says, ignoring the beauty.

The carpeted hallway muffles their march to the elevators. Nate pushes the button to call the car. John stares at the carpet at his feet. "Sorry I couldn't help."

"We'll keep working at it. You might be useful downstairs," a sly wink accompanies the jab.

The elevator arrives; the doors *swoosh* open to reveal the mirrored interior. To John, it's as if a curtain rises on a play based in the Roaring 20s. In the car a woman in a gold flapper dress and a cloche on her tight-bobbed curls leans against a man in a high-waist jacket and short pants rolled up so that John can see the brightly-colored argyle socks. John looks toward where Nate was a moment ago and sees the empty expanse of hallway. Tiny bumps pop out on his arms and march upward. *What the hell, right, I've got back-up even though I can't see him?* John steps into the elevator car and into a cloud of Gardenia and gin. The man and woman, oblivious to John's presence, are pressed together, holding each other up, and laughing.

The elevator starts down. The car glides to a stop. The doors open and the couple stumble out. John is aware of music in the air, echoes of past-conversation, and ice tinkling in forgotten cocktails. Grinning, John follows the laughing flapper and her escort. *Let's see what kind of trouble these two kids can get into.*

One. Two. Three. Six steps. A hand grips his upper arm. He stops. The flashback fades and John is blinking and starring owl-eyed at Nate. He looks around for the man and woman wanting to go back into that lively time. It is at that moment, with one foot raised in front of him, John realizes he's just about to step into the lobby Koi pond. He looks down into the amused eyes of a young girl who is looking up at him with her mouth open in amazement.

"Were you going swimming?" She's clearly in support of the action.

Her mother shushes her before John has a chance to answer, and the little girl is led away toward the restaurant. John turns to look at Nate and mouths thank you.


**8:00 p.m.**

Nate returns to the office after dropping John at his car. On Nate's desk are two messages, one from Tom Bates, and the other from Special Agent Lott. Nate picks up the one from Lott and smiles. He reaches for the phone, and dials Tom on the off chance the man was still working. The line rings and there's a click. Nate figures he'll be talking to an answering machine when Tom answers.

"Hey grammaw, d'you finish your knitting?"

Nate apologizes for not getting back with him sooner. That he was tied up with their first victim. Tom explains that he is sitting at home, relaxing, the phones forwarded to his cell and gives his okay to release the remains of the first victim to the family before launching into what he has on the second.

"Crystal Knapp; her fingerprints were in the system, served in the army from 1991 to 1995. Born July 1973, she would have been forty this year."

"Cause of death?"

"Neck broken; no water in the lungs. Still doing the toxicology. Same type of blade was used."

"It's gotta be our guy. Different result, same style."

"No fingerprints. Our guy could use gloves. I'm running the clothes for trace evidence on the off-chance something stuck instead of being washed away."

"Let me know what comes up." Nate apologizes again for the tardy call-back. He doesn't like to keep someone waiting, especially if that someone is a friend.

"Nate, I'm good. Besides, she wasn't going anywhere."

## Chapter 12
### *May 27th – 7:15 a.m.*

Freshly showered, John sleepwalks through his normal morning routine with a towel wrapped around his waist in search of something to wear. As he reaches for the handle on the closet door, the room tilts.

He's reminded of a carnival ride he used to love as a child and the pleasure and terror he felt when the bottom fell away from under his feet, and his stomach flopped. He lies on the floor with no clear recollection of how he got there. *What the hell just happened?*

Minutes pass before he attempts to prop an elbow under his body. Placing hands flat on the navy carpet he presses down and pushes to a sitting position. He puts one hand on the corner of the dresser, realizing it came within a few inches of being a disastrous way to die. One hand over the other, he "walks" himself to a standing position then leans back against the heavy piece of furniture. *A miracle folks, my towel is still firmly tucked around my nether regions.*

The room steadies itself. His head doesn't. A headache blossoms in his right temple. Squeezing eyes shut he gulps air to calm the queasy feeling in his belly, afraid the Lucky Charms will make an encore. *Pink hearts, yellow stars, and blue moons.*

His resolve lasts only a second before he loses control and scrambles to the bathroom, losing the towel along the way. He throws himself at the toilet to bring up pink hearts, yellow stars and blue moons. When John regains control, he straightens away from the porcelain bowl and goes to the mirror above the sink where a shiny-faced version of himself looks back. He rubs his cheek. Clammy. "You look like shit," he chastises his image then makes a face when the sour smell of regurgitated stomach contents reaches him. He flushes the toilet and swigs mouthwash that he spits into the sink. Then he pops three aspirin and returns to bed after a brief detour to his dresser for pajama bottoms and a t-shirt. He calls into the office to take the day off. Then turns off his phone and burrows under the bedclothes, willing the headache to go away. *Maybe I should get in to see a doctor sooner than the 12$^{th}$.*

The part of him that wishes to ignore the alarms hushes this other voice, convincing it that the headaches are nothing more than a sinus infection. *Maybe a day off work and bed rest will do the trick.* John pulls a Scarlett O'Hara and decides to put aside his. *After all tomorrow is another day.*

### 9:00 a.m.

Nate presses the End button to cut off the call before it goes to John's voicemail. He wants to talk to John in person rather than leave a message that he needs his help—again. As he places the cell phone back in his pocket he hears a high-pitched nasally greeting.

"Detective Cliffton, how you doing'?" Buddy Stanton, one of Nate's least favorite people is walking between the rows of desks headed straight towards him. The man's from New Jersey but somehow ended up on the other side of the country, God knows why. It isn't only the

50

harsh accent that annoys Nate, it's the man's entire bearing. He looks like a reporter from the forties, all rumpled and stained and smelling like onions and cigars. Nate grits his teeth behind a smile; he knows the newspaperman is on a hunting trip, looking for a juicy tip he can embellish. Nate remains seated, leaning back in his chair.

"What brings you here, Stanton?"

"A little birdie told me you have your hands full with an interesting case." The man manipulates a toothpick between his teeth while he talks. The piece of wood drifts from one side of his mouth to the other. It fascinates Nate that he doesn't lose it or choke on it.

"I hate birds; I'm more of a cat person myself." Nate casually crosses his legs straight and hooks his heals on the seat of the chair beside his desk.

"I hear you've got a couple dead bodies on your hands; 'scuse me, a body and a head of a couple of deceased tourists. Shall I tell people to stop coming to our fair city?" Stanton leans one cheek of his substantial behind and sets it on the corner of Nate's desk, ignoring the chair.

"You've got that kind of pull?"

"C'mon Detective, you're killin' me here. Give me somethin'. I hear there may be more dead bodies, er, pieces comin' at you with no clue to go on. Help me settle the hearts and minds of our readers."

"The hearts and minds of your readers will be better off not reading your paper. Don't go running off without the facts."

"Then give me some. Sounds like you got your hands full. Maybe I could help or somethin."

"You're somethin' all right, how'd you get past

51

reception?"

"I was here on another matter and thought I'd stop by to learn firsthand how you are going to protect visitors who have the misfortune to arrive and never leave."

They continue sparring. Nate tries to end the conversation and send Stanton on his way with little success until the captain comes up. "Detective Cliffton, got a minute?"

"Got to go Buddy." Nate puts his hands up in mock-surrender and jumps up to follow his supervisor out the door, ignoring the sputtering and swearing behind him.

"Everything okay with our erstwhile reporter?" Captain Bishop leads them toward his office.

"Everything's peachy."

Through the windowed wall, Nate sees a young man in a chair in front of Bishop's desk. Nate is impressed with the color combination of the suit and impeccably knotted tie—not so much, the matching vest. The man rises when Nate and the captain enter. He is almost the same height when Nate comes alongside and stops while Bishop continues around to sit behind the desk. The massive chair creaks as he settles. Bishop motions to indicate Nate and the young man should sit and Nate responds to the suggestion, lowering into the chair beside him. He gets halfway and the young man reaches out to Nate with his right hand by way of introduction. Nate rises again, but instead of shaking the young man's proffered hand he lifts an eyebrow toward the Captain.

"Nate, meet your new partner, Detective Pete Cavanaugh. He's been assigned to our department and will help you on the waterfront case. I'd like you to bring him up to speed." Bishop looks at Cavanaugh. "Put your hand down detective." Detective Cavanaugh lowers his hand and smiles.

The command hits Nate between the eyes and he abandons any thought of sitting comfortably with his boss and a guy that at first looked intriguing but now is tedious. Nate shifts so that he's facing both of them, back to the door and hands on hips. He looks at Cavanaugh as if he is a snake and will strike at any moment.

"I am pleased to be a part of your team Detective Cliffton. Heard several good things about your work, I have." This last went up as if it was a question. The entire greeting is spoken with an exceedingly British accent making Cliffton sound like its two words when the 't' is exaggerated.

Over the past few years while Nate worked under Bishop, he had been building the man up as a father figure—relying on his experience, his advice, his white hair—filling a role, but today's assignment is like a hot iron, piercing his heart.

"I don't need a partner, Captain. I've got the investigation under control. The work with the Coast Guard liaison is successful. The family of the first victim and witnesses are documented, Kominski's helping me with surveillance—"

"You've been on your own since Draper retired, Detective Cavanaugh comes to us from Los Angeles with high recommendations." The iron twists and slides deeper.

"I'm not on my own, I've got—"

Bishop's voice softens. "It's not a request, or a suggestion, it's an order, son. You're doing a hell of a job.

Consider it a favor to me that you take him under your wing. He's still got a lot to learn, and you're the best man to teach him."

Cavanaugh coughs slightly to get Nate's attention. "I understand your concerns Detective Cliffton. Give me a proper chance. You'll not regret."

*Oh just throw salt in the wound.* Deep inside Nate knows this isn't about failure or being discarded in favor of a better model, but the Captain's request and Cavanaugh's soft voice and guileless blue eyes combine to build a wall that Nate is not ready to scale. He studies Cavanaugh's face to see beyond the smile but the answers weren't there. In an act of surrender, Nate shrugs his shoulders but keeps his hands at his sides. "Welcome aboard. Follow me."

They leave Bishop's office single-file to Nate's desk. Nate motions toward an adjoining desk. "That one will be yours. It's a little dusty, and there probably isn't anything left inside that you can actually use. The guys start salvaging before the retiree gets out the door, and the seat cools down."

Nate looks at the case files in his desk drawer. A neat stack, his pad of notes on top, and pencils sharpened. Everything exactly the way he likes them. No Draper-stains or scribbles. "Here, look through these files. We'll talk in twenty minutes." He hands the files over then looks through his telephone messages, dismisses the other man.

"Care for a cuppa coffee or tea?" Cavanaugh asks.

"Coffee would be nice, maybe a nice cappuccino, with biscotti on the side." Nate knows the request is sarcastic, as if it's coming from someone else.

Detective Cavanaugh rises and leaves the room.

Nate watches the man walk away. Mary Poppins comes to mind. He sighs and looks back down at the messages, not seeing the words. Only seeing reject, Reject, REJECTION.

Ten-minutes later a fresh cup of cappuccino and chocolate chip biscotti are placed in front of him. Nate is shocked that Cavanaugh would actually fill such a frivolous order and that he could find a place that would fill the order within ten minutes.

Nate looks up at Cavanaugh, who reaches into a pocket on the inside of his jacket and pulls out a packet that contains a moistened dust cloth. Cavanaugh begins to dust the entire surface of his newly assigned work space, being extra diligent around the handles of the drawers and in the gouges that were left on the surface when a perpetrator, who everyone thought had been searched for weapons, pulled out a snub nose handgun and it went off, gouging Draper's desk, ricocheting off the metal-light-fixture in the ceiling, and lodging in a ream of paper near the printer. Once the detective is done cleaning, he finds a lone wastebasket and claims it.

Nate furtively watches as Cavanaugh scavenges a vacant chair, minus rollers, that was placed for salvage near the coffee pots and carries it over to the desk. Soon Cavanaugh is seated and pulling the case files closer. Taking a mechanical pencil and a notebook that mysteriously appears from inside his jacket Cavanaugh bends over the first reports.

Nate sits back in his chair, nibbling from one end of the biscotti and sipping the cappuccino. Nice change of pace. When he's done he wipes the crumbs off his desk onto the floor. *Change of pace for the mice, too.*

Cavanaugh neatly re-stacks the files and places his pencil parallel to the pad of paper placed to the right of the stack. Nate assumes his new partner is finished. "Care to share your thoughts," Nate says.

"It's still a bit early to form a solid analysis."

"I asked for your thoughts. An opinion, not a carved-in-stone analysis."

Cavanaugh clears his throat and begins again. "It seems the killer targets random, non-locals. Victims may be pre-selected, or one of opportunity. Opportunity to cause a disappearance. Opportunity to administer the sleeping aid. Opportunity to dispose of a body in Puget Sound."

Nate shrugs his shoulders and cocks an eyebrow, but doesn't say anything.

"I see, by your notes, you already confirmed that Natalie Sullivan did not subscribe to Thorazine. That may mean the killer supplied the dose and she ingested it prior to death. If the killer supplies the drug, the killer has access to this medication. If you wish, I could contact local medical facilities to inquire about thefts. There may also be a way to see to whom it's been prescribed."

"Worth a shot. Anything else?" Nate is grudgingly impressed.

"The signature mutilation of the right ear seems to be the killer's calling card. Unknown to us if it's a trophy, proof of the kill, or something else. Has a crime of this nature ever been recorded?"

"We've been running it through the databases, so far nothing similar has shown up. Some carvings, missing pieces, never just the right ear. I'm having Kominski compile the information, sort through it. See if there's anything I should look at."

Cavanaugh looks down at the pad of paper with his notes. Nate shoves the chart he'd made earlier across the two desks toward Detective Cavanaugh. The other man glances at it, then turns his notebook toward Nate. Sketched out on the page is a chart almost identical to Nate's.

"Interesting, okay you—" Nate's instruction is interrupted by the ring of his phone. "Cliffton" Nate's tone changes. He presses the receiver to his ear and takes up a pencil. "Thank you for calling me, Mrs. Knapp. I'm so sorry for your loss." Nate had assigned the duty of informing next-of-kin to the local police department, as was customary when the victim's family live outside his jurisdiction. "When was the last time you saw your daughter?" Nate stares at the pad of paper in front of him, concentrating on what the woman is saying to him. "She was with this Chuck Connors when she left Spokane? And when was that? How long were they going to be in Seattle?"

Nate listens a moment longer. "Mrs. Knapp, do you happen to know where they were staying, and have you heard from Chuck? Could you give me both of their phone numbers; it may help in finding him."

Nate scribbles more information. "Thank you, Mrs. Knapp. I have one more question if I might: was Crystal on any medication? No, not aspirin, something like Thorazine? It's a drug for anxiety disorders." He shakes his head "no" to Cavanaugh, who is watching him talk on the phone. "If I have further questions, at what number may I reach you? I'll let you know what we find out on this end. As soon as the body can be released, I'll contact you; and again, my condolences on your loss."

Nate hangs up, "Detective Cavanaugh, how good are you with research? Never mind answering that; I'd like you to start looking through phone records, see when the latest call or tweet was made. I'll check credit cards in both their names. See if we can figure out what Crystal Knapp and Chuck Connors were doing while in Seattle."

### 4:30 p.m.

"So we don't know where Chuck Connors is right now?" Lance is leaning against Nate's desk, back toward Detective Cavanaugh, leafing through the notes from the latest victim.

"Not sure. I checked the hotel where they were registered. They hadn't checked out, but I found nothing when the room was searched. Phone records stop towards the evening of May 17th. They sent a selfie to a friend in Spokane. Credit card records show charges around the Seattle waterfront- and one I'm especially interested in: Puget Sound Adventures." Although Nate introduced Cavanaugh as his partner when Lott came in, he's ignored him ever since and makes the entire narrative sound as if he worked everything alone.

"That's the same company the Jones family charged for the fishing trip with Natalie Sullivan, right?" Lott asks.

"Might be worth a trip out there to have a talk. Hey, Chuck Connors," Nate chuckles. "Parents must have been fans of the old *Rifleman* show."

Nate glances at Lott, then around him toward a

quiet Cavanaugh. "*Rifleman*? Anyone?" Blank stares from both men.

"Crystal's body was found on the west side of Whidbey Island, could indicate a specific dumping zone. The currents and wind direction indicate it could be the same as our first victim." There was Lott, the water guy.

"Might be good to go back out there?" Nate muses. "See if we can find Chuck." This is a first for Nate, bodies in the water. He isn't sure if another dive will bring up Chuck, or was Chuck the murderer and on his way to another state. Cost versus benefit. Would it be worth it?

Lance stands, returning the file to Nate. "I'll talk to my boss about scheduling a launch. Let you know what she says. Get some beauty sleep, Detective Cliffton." He winks and walks out of the office leaving nothing between Nate and his new partner but dust motes floating around in empty space.

Chapter 13

*May 28th – 8:15 a.m.*

The warrant to search the Puget Sound Adventures computers would be waiting on Nate's desk this morning. He feels the itch. Impatient to look inside, see if the employees smile and nod, friendly like, but behind the red velvet—*Don't pay attention to the man behind the curtain*—evil lurks. It's a fishing trip. Nate appreciates the irony, however he's late after spending last night with Lance. He strides into the building thirty-minutes later than his usual seven-thirty and by the time the elevator arrives at the first floor to scoop up other government workers and spit them out on every floor, he's a total of forty-five minutes late. He walks into the office just as his phone starts a tinny-sounding version of the 2006 hip-hop song by Fergie, *London Bridge*. He fumbles in his jacket to silence the cell phone and surreptitiously glances at Pete who is slowly turning towards him. Nate knows when realization hits the other man's eyes and Pete holds his cell phone above his head and deliberately clicks the end button that the choice of ring tone for his partner is no longer his little secret.

The club track silenced, Nate feels warmth spread from his shirt collar to the top of his head. He ignores the roll of Pete's eyes and focuses on what he's saying.

"The warrant arrived this morning. There's a manager who oversees scheduling and is the face of the company on shore. He should be there now, they open at eight." Pete adds emphasis to the last word.

"Well, all right then, what are we waiting for?"

Pete's right eyebrow arches and he opens his mouth. Nate turns to leave, cutting him off and hiding the satisfied smirk on his face. Nate retraces his steps toward the elevator.

### *10:00 a.m.*

In the Puget Sound Adventures office, a four-by-four shed that resembles a portable bathroom, a sandy-haired young man behind the counter with Darius Adamya etched on a nameplate on the desk in front of him asks what he can do for them.

Nate's first impression puts Adamya in the category of college graduate, who decides to turn his back on the corporate grime and meander into an itinerant life on the waterfront. Contrary to his casual posture and worn clothing, Adamya appears to spend a lot of time and focus at a gym. He is free of facial hair with intense eyes—one blue the other hazel, almost yellow. Nate recalls the doctor's term for it, Heterochromia. The effect gives Adamya the look of a predator. *Wonder what's his story.* "Adamya, that's Indian, Suquamish?"

"I think it means *difficult* in some language, but my parents were never part of the Indian culture here in Seattle."

They settle on Darius; Nate introduces himself and Pete and serves the warrant exuding community spirit and camaraderie.

"What's this about? I'm just the manager here. I'm going to have to call the owner of Puget Sound."

61

"That would be Willis Playford III of San Francisco?" Pete says.

"Yeah, I just run the place, answer the phones, and take the customer's money. The owner hasn't been up here in a couple years, just throws his attorneys at us if he needs anything. Here's his card—quite the entrepreneur, collects businesses and properties around the world. Don't know if he ever gets a chance to enjoy any of his things." Adamya breaks out in a shark's smile, all teeth and empty eyes. Nate takes the business card out of his hand and passes it to Pete.

"You may call Mr. Playford to let him know we're here, but that won't stop us from looking around. The warrant gives access to your computers—"

"There's just the one."

Nate glances at his wristwatch. "Tech team should be here soon. If you would be so kind as to step out from behind the desk and follow Detective Cavanaugh outside, he has a few questions for you."

Nate allows Darius to pass, and once the two men exit the building, slides around behind the desk. Gloved hands sift through the contents of desk drawers. Nothing of interest. Nate would rather find the schedule that lists passengers on fishing excursions. See if the same boat and captain took out both victims. See if there was a commonality there. He flips through the pages of a planner that was open to today's date. Carefully recorded were the name of a boat, then a.m. or p.m. alongside and a name. Nate could only guess at the name. He'd talk to Darius about it. He finishes and walks outside just as the CSI truck pulls into the parking area. Nate walks over to the driver.

"There's a computer inside that I want you to go

through. I'm looking for a schedule for the month of May. Make copies of the files to take back to the office. I'll be over there if you need anything." He nods toward the pier.

Nate heads over to Pete and Darius, who are sitting on a park bench on the pier that runs in front of the PSA office. "You get the name of the boats PSA owns?" he asks Pete.

"*The Mariner, The Sounder,* and *The Mosquito* occupy Piers 47 through 49. *The Mosquito's* out right now. Another, *The Mermaid,* hasn't been out in months. It's up on blocks near the warehouse, the pole barn over there." Pete points toward a metal structure a short distance from them.

"What time will—?"

"About one." Darius' answer is clipped. Providing just enough information but the friendly expanse has left the building.

Nate props one foot on the edge of the bench and leans on his thigh. He's got Darius' full attention. "Do you record the names of your customers and which boat they go out on?"

"I'd only have the name of the person paying."

"What are the names listed in the planner inside?"

"Which guy is captaining which boat and when."

Nate listens to the staccato response and scribbles in his notepad. "Do you ever go out on the boats, Darius, or are you pretty much confined to the office?"

Darius frowns in response, looking down. He draws out the response like they had all day. "I'll join a boat if, like, it's missing a crew member because someone's on vacation or sick. When that happens the office phone can be forwarded to my cell number." Then he quickly diminishes his involvement. "Doesn't happen often."

"So only random outings."

"Yeah. Nothing scheduled. Usually last minute."

"When was the last time you were out?"

"Last week. Not sure which day."

Nate puts his notepad away, watching as Darius fidgets. "We should be done within the hour. You can take an early lunch. If you leave, make sure we've got your contact information."

"You never said what this was about."

Nate looks into his eyes. One blue, one hazel. "Have Mr. Playford contact me, I'll explain everything to him."

Darius huffs and gets up. It looks like he wants to say something but instead he turns and walks away across the parking lot. Halfway across the lot, he's got the cell phone to his ear.

"Did you get his contact information?" Nate watches Pete finish scribbling. Pete nods.

Nate sighs and shifts around to look out at the water. "Couldn't see anything out of place in there. Guess I was hoping for a flashing arrow pointing to the killer."

"If the killer is in fact affiliated with PSA." Pete closes his notepad and stands beside him.

Nate squares his shoulders. "If you need to dump a body in Puget Sound, you gotta have a boat."


*11:30 a.m.*

"Hey stranger." The waitress grins and nods in my direction as I head to a stool at the section of the counter where a mug of coffee sits waiting for me.

"Thanks, Doll."

"Been out fishing today?"

"Not today. There's a tour out, but they didn't need me."

"Aw, honey, I need you." The waitress is in her fifties but I smile at her, enjoying the attention. Looking around the crowded restaurant I lean over the counter so only she can hear me.

"This place is crawling with tourists. What did you do, put out a sign that said free coffee for non-residents?"

"I don't know what it is, but it's been like this since six this morning. Are you having the usual?" she asks, waiting for my nod of agreement.

I oblige, and she slowly waddles around to the other end of the counter to serve another customer, white orthopedic shoes squeaking on the tile. I sip my coffee, listening to the roar of conversations and the low rumble from the traffic outside. Two televisions mounted high yell at each other in the name of entertainment—ESPN and a non-stop news station.

My grilled three-cheese sandwich with Mama Lil's sweet-hot peppers and homemade tomato jam and a side of fries arrive. Half the food is gone when my phone chirps. I pull it out of my jeans pocket, looking at the one-sentence text message. Displeased and restless I finish the coffee, pull out a few dollar bills, and throw them on the counter. Sliding off the stool, I head for the door through the laughing and shouting tourists.

## 1:00 p.m.

Mike Flynn has reached the end of his rope. No, that's not it. Mike Flynn is at the end of his mini-fishing-vacation that was supposed to refresh and revive. Three days were not long enough to wash off the tension of the corporate tightrope or the constant worry of rejection from clients and bosses. He knew the wolves were nipping at his heel. Newer, younger, fresher coworkers were more than willing to take over at the first sign of weakness.

He trudges down the hallway to the motel's registration desk to check-out, worn luggage following obediently on weary wheels. Squeak. Squeak. Squeak. His shoulders in a perpetual slouch, like a comma, as if he's been harnessed for the past forty years beneath a heavy yoke like an ox, toiling the land. Truth is the slouch didn't appear until after his wife's death. Something as unforeseen as a brain aneurism—silent but deadly—and she was gone. Connie, his rock, the constant airstream beneath his outstretched arms, was gone and he is having trouble keeping afloat. Before her death he envisioned working toward a nice little retirement apartment on a beach in Florida. He'd come in after a round of golf in his pastel polo and she'd be smiling at him, holding out a beer, the sun sprinkling her face with freckles and nature's blush.

Connie and Mike Flynn were foster parents to several children and played Mr. And Mrs. Claus at their church where homeless families gathered for a holiday meal. This past Christmas the Clauses didn't make it to

66

church and he'd spent the month of December planning her funeral.

This morning he's nursing a hangover and he doesn't know if he's more disappointed in the fact that his vacation is over, or that he's let down angel-Connie by over-indulging. *Please forgive me Connie dear, I miss you so.*

Shuffling through the entrance he drag-carries the bag around to the trunk of a beat-up Mazda. He and Connie always planned to buy a new car with his pension money when the time came. That time loomed further off in the future because the thought of retiring alone scared him. He lifts the bag into the trunk and slams the lid, wincing as the sound assails his ear drums and brittle skull. He walks around and opens the car door, squeezing his corporate ass and slight paunch behind the steering wheel. He mops sweat off his face with his handkerchief, smelling tequila on the damp cloth.

"Mikey, time to get home and sober up your bright eyes and fluff out your bushy tail," he mutters as he jams the car key into the ignition and twists.

The engine catches, coughs, then chugs, sounding as if it hasn't decided whether it wants to go home or stay here for a while. Finally it catches and growls and he puts the car in gear and inches out of the parking lot to join commuters on their way to lunch or work or a bar, if they are lucky. *I'm just kidding Connie.*

The car travels two blocks before a final gasp. Silence. He coasts to the curb and puts it in park. He tries the key again—nothing. A second try. He isn't going anywhere. *Sigh.* Mike slumps forward, touching his head to the lukewarm plastic of the steering wheel where he remains for a few seconds, eyes closed, trying to find some momentum to get out of the car.

The engine clicks as it cools. The clicks are timed perfectly to the pounding in his head. He fantasizes about a three-piece jazz band, playing a fast-tempo version of Kenny G's *Going Home*.

"Shit." The one word seems to describe how he's feeling, and the situation, and his life in general; it's so appropriate he repeats the word, louder, "SHIT."

"Need any help?"

Mike gasps at the muffled statement, startled to see a man standing beside the car and staring into his side window with eyes that seem to drill right through the glass and into his forehead. A bead of sweat forms and slowly traces its way down the right side of his face.

Mike rolls the window down, "My car won't start." He looks at the compelling eyes of the man standing bent forward, slightly, with his arms resting on the top of the car as if laying claim to the vehicle and all those inside. Mike leans away from the window. There's something disquieting about the eyes looking at him, and there was something familiar about the man.

"Do I know you?"

"I don't know, do you?"

The response is both playful and challenging. Mike can't quite put his finger on why an alarm is sounding in his head. Mike forces a smile on his face as he looks up at the helpful stranger who looks like he might know something about cars. With a slow smile the stranger reaches for the door handle and opens the door of the car like a charismatic boy hoping the chivalrous gesture will get him to second or third base. Mike fumbles with his seatbelt and climbs out. Standing chin-to-chin, Mike suddenly remembers where he's seen the guy before.

"Now I remember. You worked the fishing charter I went out on." Recovering his manners he sticks out a hand to formally introduce himself, "I'm Mike, Mike Flynn."

"Pleased to meet up with you again, Mike Flynn." The slow smile playing around the man's lips never gets to flat eyes. The effect was like looking at a house with the lights on in all the rooms on the first floor and the upper floors dark. Hands clasped in greeting, Mike feels the cool dryness of the man's palm and the strength in his grasp. Mike glances down to see a leather belt and a flash, as if there is a gun or a knife attached to it, hidden by the man's polo shirt. The uneasy feeling returns, and Mike's brow puckers as he realizes the man didn't provide a name. The stranger doesn't seem to notice and turns to walk toward the front of Mike's car. Mike follows, staying a couple feet behind. The man raises the hood, secures it with a metal rod, then tests some of the connections, and checks the oil.

"Could be the starter, battery doesn't appear to be corroded, but it could be dead, too." The man seems indifferent, sounding bored. Mike figures he could have bent over the engine himself to come up with as much as this guy.

"I could give you a lift to wherever you want to go unless you've got jumper cables on you. I don't. That's my car right behind yours."

Helpful to a point. Mike looks back at the light brown non-descript vehicle. *It looks in worse shape than my car.* He hesitates for one simple reason. The guy scares the crap out of him. "I better stay with my car, you know, so they can find me. I'll just call for a tow."

"I could take you to a mechanic right down the road. You could talk to them, and they could ride back with you."

The desire to get home overwhelms him, and Mike wavers. The offer seems sincere and Mike isn't paying AAA or any other company for roadside assistance. *If it's just down the street, I could stand to ride in the same car with him for a few minutes. He's probably just a normal guy. What could be the worse that happens?*

Mike nods his head to accept. A horn blares. Mike jumps straight into the air before turning to see the tow truck pull alongside his car with a guy that's all smiles sitting in the driver's seat.

"Hey, look. This is probably the guy from that mechanic shop down the str—." Mike turns to the fishing-charter guy still standing in front of the hood. The look in the man's odd eyes stops him cold. Mike shuffles back a few steps. Throwing a half-hearted thank you over his shoulder he scurries over to his new benefactor.

"Oh man, am I happy to see you. Can you tow me to your shop?"

"No problem, hop in." Mike runs around to the passenger side to climb in and the tow truck is maneuvered in front of Mike's vehicle. The driver gets out, "I'll just be a minute."

Mike looks in the driver side mirror. He sees the fishing-charter guy walking back to his car. Right this minute felt like a time when he was a kid hanging out with his neighborhood friends. The other kids tried to convince him to enter a house they all thought was haunted through the old-fashioned outside cellar doors. There wasn't a lock on the wooden doors and no one was home. Mike almost went with them but at the last minute changed his mind and climbed a tree in the yard next door. The other boys went into the cellar. They were still in there when the owners returned, the car gliding up the driveway to park beside the open cellar door. What followed was detention for his friends. This felt like that time long ago, like he'd just escaped detention.

"Connie, pumpkin, I don't think I'd of made it back home with that guy."

## Chapter 14 – Reflections of a Killer

I knew at an early age that I was different from my siblings. Born in Seattle, my dad moved us all over the country pursing promotions. During my *formative years* I studied my sisters and the kids at school for clues so I'd fit it. Mimic their actions and emotions. Develop my acting skills. One week I'd be bully-Jason, jutting my jaw out and daring the smaller boys to fight. The next week I'd be bookworm-Norman, politely holding the doors for the girls and sitting quietly in class listening to the teacher. I had a lot of friends, but I only wanted to hang out with them when I was social-butterfly-Olivia. Then I'd smile and compliment all of the kids, even nose-picking, booger-eating Christina.

When I was seven I found a spider web attached between the house siding and a pillar on the front porch of our Dalton, Georgia, home. I decided to name my eight-legged friend, Charlotte, after a book my mom read to me and my sisters. Every day I'd throw flies and ants into the web to watch the spider skitter out and claim its meal. That spider grew fat over summer, but by the time the leaves turned I set it afire with an orange Bic lighter.

When I was fifteen I put Dora, my sister's hamster, into a canning jar, filled it with water, and screwed the lid on tight, watching the hamster's claws skitter around on the glass trying to force its way out. Then its whole body shuttered as it breathed in the water. I carefully dried the dead rodent with my mom's hair dryer and laid it down in its cage for Shelly to find when she returned from her sleepover. The family dog met a similar fate only no water was involved but I don't think that meant it suffered less than Dora. Spot's probably still buried in the backyard of our Lansing, Michigan, home where I secretly placed him one latch-key afternoon.

When I was sixteen playing with a kid my age across the street from where we lived in Florida, we found some matches. I talked him in to taking them outside. We started burning ants and silk worms, watching them blacken and curl into themselves and I wondered what a person would look like burning to a crisp like these insects. Dustin's mom screamed louder than Dustin when she saw him stumble around in the backyard waving an arm engulfed in flames. She threw Dustin to the ground and wrapped him in a tablecloth. Once she had the fire under control and sat up to dial 911, she noticed me. It was too late to rearrange my face to look like frightened-Sam or helpful-Jodi. I went back home and turned on SpongeBob Squarepants. That night my parents heard from Dustin's dad.

That was the year my parents took me to see a counselor specializing in conduct and personality therapy. Twenty-three months later, the counselor told them I had an enduring deviate pattern of behavior across both my social and personal situations, and they should seek professional psychiatric help in getting me the correct treatment. What the what? I played remorseful-Amy and they found a doctor that would prescribe the proper medication.

When I was eighteen I moved out. I'd enrolled in a community college to experience college life—think of air quotes—and moved into a dorm. There I was supposed to study business administration, but instead I studied all the different personalities around me. Slut-Mollie, Jock-Cameron, Druggie-Max, and Smug-Professor Dahlquist. I visited my folks on rare weekends when I needed a good meal or to do laundry. My mom would cry when I left, asking me to visit more often. I didn't. My dad would hand me a hundred dollars and beg me to continue treatments with a doctor he'd found. I didn't. They both prayed I'd graduate, find someone to spend the rest of my life with, have children, and basically become a normal son. I didn't.

## Chapter 15
### *May 31ˢᵗ – 1:00 p.m.*

Derek and his partner Mark, along with five of their friends, drive up to Seattle for the weekend with the specific goals to drink fresh-brewed coffee at an original Starbucks in Pike Place Market, visit the top of the Space Needle, and spend an afternoon on a charter-fishing boat in the hope that the evening will end with fresh-fish tacos. The weekend-weather predictions although not ideal were okay for fishing and partying with a little sunbathing thrown in for the warm-blooded in the group.

Friday with its sunshine and warmth is the day they decide to take out a charter boat for an afternoon. They pick a company that offers to clean all fish caught during the trip. An hour after boarding, the boys are well on their way to a merry celebration. The charter-boat crew tolerates the drunken group making sure none of them fall overboard. Both of the seamen are average height and wiry. Both are cute in a rugged sort of way with laugh lines around their eyes that show whiter than the rest of their tanned faces. Both pay Derek a certain amount of attention so that he imagines he is the saucy romance novel in-between two muscled bookends.

It makes perfect sense to Derek when his friends are otherwise occupied with fishing or drinking, and Mark takes a snooze on the bow of the boat that he flirts. Thirty-one going on twenty, Derek sways his slim hips and poses in front of one and then the other crew member as he saunters between them on the deck. Pursing his lips, he plays with a curl in his auburn hair. Talking and smiling and crinkling his hazel eyes whenever one of them comments back.

Derek finally focuses on the one with the intense eyes. He leans in close and invites him to hook-up at a bar that evening. *I can do that.* The guy agrees.

### 6:30 p.m.

Derek looks out of the sliding door of the room he shares with Mark to see what his partner and the others are doing this early evening. Mark is sprawled on a lounge chair, mouth agape, fast asleep in spite of the sounds coming out of the iPod dock speakers and the giggles and conversation of his friends as they polish each other's toe nails. Mark looks so cute in his black and white Speedo, with the start of a sunburn showing on his left inner thigh. Derek wavers staring at his lover. Sheepish.

They've been together for five years. They were good years, and Derek knew he should be satisfied, but there was a birthday looming, which brought on twinges of depression and feelings of dissatisfaction.

Normally he'd be out there with them, drinking and dancing, and trying to be the center of attention. One of his friends waves a martini glass above his head and calls to him.

"Yoo-hoo, Derek, come on in the water's fine, plenty of *martoonis* to go around." They all laugh including Derek.

"I can't. I'm going down for my massage. Tell Mark—" Derek hesitates. "Tell Mark I'll see him later."

Then he blows a kiss to the group and heads for the lobby. He slips out of the hotel.


*7:30 p.m.*

Derek is the first to arrive, and he selects a table where he can watch the door, while keeping an eye on the dancer gyrating in front of him. The bar is called the Sea Unicorn, and the interior design is tacky chic. The sign out front depicts a seahorse with a unicorn's horn, and the floor show consists of twinks covered in netting and strategically placed sea shells on the raised platforms arranged throughout the room dancing to Lady Gaga or Madonna.

He turns back to the table to sip his drink and sees his image in the mirrored column beside him. He watches as the mirror twin reaches a hand to adjust an errant auburn curl. Giving his appearance the once-over with a critical eye, he turns away from the mirrored testimony to his increasing age.

*It takes a lot of product to look this young and beautiful.* He sips and resumes his watch.

When the guy from the charter walks in, Derek notices right away that he paid special attention to his appearance, and even has a smooth face from a clean shave; he looks handsome in a rough-Daniel-Craig-sort-of-way, a little hard around the edges. *Not the usual type I'm attracted to, but I'm bored and in the mood for something a little rougher.*

The guy from the charter approaches the table, and when he sees Derek's drink is almost empty he leans in close and asks if he can buy him another.

"Pomegranate martini, if you please, but there will be someone here to take our order soon, just have a seat." Derek pats the chair beside him.

"No problem, I'll be right back." The Daniel-Craig-look-alike heads over to the bar to fill the order.

*You're going to get laid*, Derek's conscience sing-songs in his head.

After his second martini Derek feels light-headed and needs to get out of the bar for a breath of fresh air. His male friend is happy to oblige him, steering him towards the door and then to the parking lot. They are almost to a light-brown vehicle near the back of the lot.

"Oh, I feel strange."

"Here, we're almost to my car. I can drive you any place you like."

*There's something wrong with me.* Derek's head fills with ragged panting like a tired, old dog. He realizes the sound is his own breathing. Derek leans into the man holding onto him, staring at the vehicle and willing the darkness to recede as he struggles to view the world through a black tunnel.


## 10:30 p.m.

Hazel eyes flutter open. *What hit me ... one minute I'm having a few drinks, no more than any other night, the next I'm ... where am I?* Derek smells the familiar scents of the Seattle waterfront, but there are other smells he can not readily identify, and he tries to get his bearings. *I'm wet and naked.* He shivers.

*Did I pass out? Of course I passed out. How embarrassing. Well this evening got kinky. Where am I? Did he drop me off at the hotel? Is Mark pissed?* He lies quietly a moment more, gathering himself. He starts to sit up but stops when Daniel Craig appears above him.

Before Derek can flirt, he catches a glint of light out of the corner of his eyes. A flash and then a comet trail, the light arches downward. It feels like his body is encased in cement, movement slow and laborious, raising an arm to defend himself. Knowing full well he is too late. Only time for one quick lament.

*Mark, I'm sorry.*


**1:30 a.m.**


The message is brief, delivered through satellites and cell towers to the phone of a person I have never met, nor ever intend to meet, a person with similar interests and talents. The picture I attach shows seven small objects crusted with brown flakes. Six of them are gray, the final one slightly pink and curled like a flower with a strand of auburn hair clinging to the underside. I smile as I push send. Then I throw the disposable over the side.

Nate thumps his desktop in a wobbly rendition of Wipe Out by the Beach Boys. So far his list of suspects is like a grocery list you put together on the day after payday. Everyone's on it—family, friends, employees of Puget Sound Adventures, passersby—soup to nuts. So far nothing ties to anything and no one seems to have a motive, and no murder weapon has surfaced. He glares at the phone willing Lance to call him to let him know when the next search-and-retrieval is scheduled. Lance said his department had tip-toed through the budget issues and all that was left to do was get the thing on the calendar.

Nate looks at Pete who is doing the arduous task of sifting through the Puget Sound Adventures' employee records to see if anyone has a criminal past — parking ticket, assault, the usual. Nate didn't want to spend time on the computer so he used his trump-partner card. That was one advantage to being assigned a new partner and maintaining the lead investigator role. Draper, Nate's last partner, had lorded-it-over him the whole time they worked together so Nate not only got all the grunt work, he got all the racially-inappropriate, gender-biased, and homophobic jibes as well.

The office is unusually quiet, as if everyone ran out during a fire drill, aside from Nate's drumming. When Pete grunts, Nate jumps. He frowns at his nervous reaction and growls in a tone to match the frown. "What have you got?"

"Captains Kessler, Whitehead, and Fitzgerald appear to be clean. I've found nothing so far to suggest

80

otherwise."

"That's it? That's all you got in—," Nate looks up at the clock hanging above the office door. "Two hours?"

"I may have something on one of the boat-crew members, Richie Carson."

"Go on."

"I was going through the names, checking motor records, arrests, etc., looking them up on Facebook and other social media—."

"Just the cliffnotes."

Pete waggles his head at Nate. "I did find some employees who had joined one group or another."

"Bottom line, Pete?"

Pete flinches. Primly he positions his mechanical pencil, first one side of the keyboard, then the other. "On Richie Carson's social website there are several messages—an argument with Corinna. The last thing she says is to imply his use of drugs. The exact wording." Leaning into the computer screen, Pete reads, "*Have you forgotten to take your meds? You need to chill.*" He straightens and wiggles the knot in his tie. "And then she uses vulgar language."

"That'll give us a chance to bring him in. Got an address?"


*11:30 a.m.*


"Richie, tell me where you were the night of May seventeenth." Nate sits opposite a man who smells so strongly of fish that Nate has to force himself to keep his hand at his side and not over his nose.

Richie slouches back in the chair. Eyes dart—first one face then the other, then one corner of the table to the other. His brow is one long line over his nose—a uni-brow furrowed and distrustful. "The seventeenth, what day was that?" The answer sullen and short.

Nate tries again. "Where were you the evening of Friday, May seventeenth?"

"Probably out on a charter. That's where I usually am. Then clean up, dinner, home. Sometimes a bar." His shoulders go up and down, dismissive.

"I suppose a priest, a rabbi, and two Irish nuns will swear to you being in a bar that night." A light in Nate's eyes dance. He'd bet his next paycheck this guy hasn't cleaned up in a while. Nate waits for a response to the sarcastic statement.

"Well, I usually hang out at the same places. You can ask around."

Nate sighs, looking at the calluses on Richie's hands. He waits.

Richie continues to fidget. "It was a few weeks ago. Don't ask me what I had for lunch yesterday."

Nate pulls two photos out of his file and places them just out of reach in front of Richie. "Do you know either of these women? Or this man?" Natalie, Crystal and Chuck smile up at Richie.

Richie bends down toward the photos, squinting. "I don't know him. I don't remember seeing this one," he points at Crystal. Then he taps on Natalie's photo. "She seems familiar, but I'm not sure. Could just be the blonde hair. Why? Who are these people?"

82

"Two of them are dead, the third's missing."

Richie pushes back from the table. Nate jerks his head at Pete to move closer to the door. With a look of horror on his face, Richie is finally awake and taking notice. "Wait a minute, I didn't do anything. I'm not a killer."

"You're not. Do you take any drugs, Richie?" Nate returns the photos to his folder.

"I don't do—I don't do drugs." He's sullen, hunched forward and looking at the floor between his shoes.

"Why'd Corinna mention them on your Facebook page?"

"Facebook. Hah. What a joke. Stupidest thing I ever did was sign up." Richie sneers. "She made me do it. Corinna talked me into starting a page, like it would make things better between us."

"She a girlfriend?"

Richie doesn't answer. His shoulders rise in an indifferent motion.

"Why did she tell you to take your drugs? What drug was she referring to?"

"Something I've taken since I was in my teens." Richie mutters into his chest. "I had some problems with coping. My parents got me on it." He shrugs again, "I still take it."

"Rich, its okay if I call you Rich?" Nate continues without waiting for a response. "You could help us out by helping us understand why a guy like you doesn't seem to have any girlfriends or boyfriends, can't tell us exactly where you were or who you were with the night of the seventeenth, has personality problems, and lives alone in an apartment without a cat or dog for company."

"Very sad," Pete murmurs.

Richie seems confused, his eyes searching the floor tiles.

"I'm a simple guy."

"What drug do you still take?"

"Thorazine." One word, spoken quietly.

"Did anyone know about the Thorazine? Anyone at work?" A thought occurs to Nate.

"I s'pose so. It's on my application."

"Darius Adamya?"

"Yeah, maybe, I don't know. Probably. And the owner. Why?"

"You ever take the pills into work?"

"No, I keep 'em at home. I don't carry any around."

"Rich, you wouldn't mind if we looked around your apartment, would you?"

"No, why should I mind? But hey—"

Nate quickly motions to Pete who exits, and he turns to Richie with an offer. "Let me grab you a sandwich and something to drink." Then he follows Pete out into the hall, closing the door on Richie's question. *Do I need a lawyer? I didn't do anything wrong.*

Captain Bishop walks up to Nate and Pete and nods toward the interrogation room. "You think this is your man?"

"Not sure," Nate says. "Just fishing today, no pun intended. He just gave me permission to check out his apartment."

"Real sharp cookie, huh? Keep me posted." Bishop

continues down the hall.

Nate heads in the direction of his office, Pete trailing. A uniform passes and Nate stops him. "Hey, could you get the guy in there a sandwich and a Coke," Nate's thumb points in the direction of the interrogation room. "It'd be a big favor to me." The officer nods and Nate adds, "Don't take it to him right away. Give me an hour."

### 1:30 p.m.

Nate stares around at a jumbled pigsty also known as Richie Carson's apartment. Pulling on gloves, he is careful to stay out of the way of the CSI technicians who are there to snap photos and take possession of anything that looks like a weapon. Nate walks over to the bathroom and Pete starts to follow. Nate stops and turns, hand coming up to Pete's chest. You take notes of what CSI is doing."

"Seriously?" Pete's face flushes.

Nate nods and continues to the door of the bathroom where he looks in. *Glad I've got my gloves and booties.* Then he sees the toilet and almost calls Pete to have him take over. Searching the room he finds a bottle of pills lying on the counter beside the sink. He looks inside. There were approximately twenty pills. *Get him through June.* He places the bottle in an evidence bag and performs a cursory search of the cabinets and bins holding dirty laundry, trash, and a used condom, *Someone's still coming around, Corinna?* The one thing he didn't see was a weapon or sharp blade.

Nate walks out of the bathroom as CSI finishes in

85

the bedroom. "Anything?"

The technician shakes his head. Nate spends another half hour avoiding Pete before giving up and heading back to the office.

### 4:30 p.m.

Nate's lost a little pep. He trudges back to his desk to close up for the day. Before he leaves, Nate orders Pete to get the list of usual hangouts from Richie and to release him. Not worth the time and effort of keeping him any longer.

## Chapter 17

*June 5ᵗʰ – 1:00 p.m*

The Coast Guard cutter slices through the water toward the coordinates used for the first search-and-retrieval. A relatively shallow sill with a mean depth of 115 feet, the cutter will use sonar equipment in the area moving toward Whidbey Island where Crystal's body washed up. Nate is quiet. He's feeling like a failure. He's been on the case since May 14ᵗʰ and he still didn't have anything to go on. John hasn't been any help. Nate wasn't mad or anything, just disappointed. And then there's Pete, his albatross. Having Pete trail around behind him hasn't improved his attitude, although his morning coffee has improved. The guy was trying, Nate knew that. And Pete was more patient than Nate would have been in the same situation. *I'm an ass.*

Nate shakes his thoughts off like a dog shakes off a bath. His eyes return to the water. It sparkles in the sun as it flies off the bow. Nate's head is low, nose tucked into the front of his jacket. Insulating himself from everyone on board. He spies on Pete. An expensive-looking scarf is neatly tucked around his neck. He's wearing ear muffs. *Ear muffs!* A silly ensemble given the June date. Lott is sitting upright with the collar of his shirt open and his jacket on the bench beside him, embracing the wind. Near their destination, Lott goes to the locker area to change. Nate's eyes follow his movements. Lott phoned Nate late yesterday to let him know when today's event was scheduled. He suggested they get together for dinner. Nate refused. The relationship with the charming SA is beginning to stifle commitment-phobe Nate.

### 3:00 p.m.

The team finds something. Nate and Pete move toward the side as the cage comes up. The clank of metal sets off Nate's stretched nerves, quivering in time to the clicks. Water and seaweed streams from the metal contraption as it rises over the side and settles on the deck. Nate is staring at the center when a commotion draws his attention.

"Shark!"

The men are still dog-paddling in the water taking their time getting into the boat. The cry motivates them. A rescue basket drops into the water and another Coast Guard officer suits up, prepared to dive in with an anti-shark weapon. Another officer scrambles onto a raised platform with a rifle.

Nate's heart is in his throat as he tries to see where the shark is in relation to Lance. The shark appears to be approximately five feet long and is slowly making a half circle. Taking it's time. More curious that hungry. Time stands still. Tense seconds tick away as if each were taking an hour to pass by. Nate doesn't start breathing again until Lance is safely into the basket. Then he and the rest of the men are pulled aboard. Emergency over. The tension in the air dissipates as everyone gawks at the shark from the deck.

"Well, that was exciting." Pete says, rolling his eyes.

Nate's teeth are still clenched, he looks at Lance. The other man winks. Nate's jaw relaxes and he shakes his head, a grin thawing his face. He turns to the reason they were out there. In the center of the cage is a man's head, minus the right ear.

"I'll bet this is Chuck."

# Chapter 18
## *June 8ᵗʰ – 8:00 a.m.*

Nate's morning is not going well after a short phone conversation with his sister that left him feeling more frustrated than connected. He arrives in the office at the usual time to Pete Cavanaugh and a Styrofoam cup of fresh-brewed coffee. Instead of bringing a smile, this small act seems to put him in a deeper funk. Nate thanks the man by way of telling him he didn't need to keep supplying him with coffee. Now Nate sits hunched over the cup as if it is a campfire and he is stranded in a snow-covered wilderness listening to the wolves howl just out of view.

"Cliffton," the one word response to the ringing flies at the phone.

"Detective Cliffton? This is Sergeant Lloyd over at Missing Persons. You wanted us to contact you with any new calls. We've had a couple that came in this past week."

"Yeah Sergeant, what have you got?"

"One is a fifty-eight year old woman, Charlene Hawkins. Husband reported her missing night before last. An officer looked into it, and found her after checking with—"

"Why are you bringing up that one? I want missing."

"Geesh, it was a funny story."

Pressing the pencil and scratching out the notes he started, the graphite obliterating the words beneath, he tries to keep the irritation out of his voice as he interrupts. "You had another one?"

"Yeah, this one is still open. A guy calls in to report

his boyfriend, a Derek Southwell, has gone missing."

"Okay and you checked into it?"

"Yeah. They were visiting Seattle last weekend. But get this: he waits until yesterday before calling it in. Apparently what held him up was the text message he got from lover-boy saying it was over and never to call him again. I asked him why now, why did he wait? You know what his response was: he said the boyfriend's mommy had called to talk to her missing son."

Nate's intuition tells him this case is relevant and not just his feverish way of finding evidence. "Give me his contact information, Sergeant, and could you send me a copy of your file. You said they were visiting Seattle. From where?"

"They live in San Francisco. Figures."

Nate ignores the off-hand comment, and repeats his request for contact information. When Sergeant Lloyd promises to send the file copy, Nate hangs up. *Derek Southwell, where are you right now?* A spark goes off inside Nate's head and his vision narrows on the words, "text message."


*4:00 p.m.*


"Thank you for traveling here to talk to me so soon. Your friend has a private plane?" Nate places his hand on the wooden chair beside his desk and nods downward indicating to Mark Campbell that he could sit.

"You said it had something to do with Derek." Mark said. "Of course I'd come; is he all right? Have you

91

found him?" The on-again, off-again partner of Derek "Cherry Bomb" Southwell looks to be between the ages of thirty-four and forty, average height, a slight roll over his belt—he'd have to worry about that soon, more sit-ups at the gym—and brown hair and eyes. When Nate called, Mark immediately said he'd come in person. Now, sitting before Nate with red-rimmed eyes, he is clearly upset, his body as rigid as the hard chair beneath him. A tattered and slightly used tissue clutched in his hands.

"We haven't located him, but we're doing all we can to find him and bring you piece of mind. Derek's disappearance may connect to a case I'm working on. I thought we could talk, maybe help each other."

"You think he's okay, right? You don't think anything's happened to him, do you?" Mark's shoulders are bunched, as if the June weather does not warm him.

Nate doesn't have any toasty news to tell him. "I don't know the answer to that question."

"I gave all the information to someone in Missing Persons. Don't you people talk?" Mark's voice cracks.

The corners of Nate's mouth curl in a sympathetic gesture. "Believe me the information you already provided we still have, and I've seen it."

"All right. Why did you call me?"

"I want to focus on the text message and ask you about details of your stay," Nate says. "It's the way I do business. Start at the beginning and move forward. I have the name of the hotel you stayed in, tell me the activities you did while you were here."

Mark sniffles and blows into the already dirty tissue.

Nate holds a wastebasket underneath the hand that clutches the spent paper square, but Mark seems not to notice.

"Okay, well we came up on a Thursday for a four-day weekend, Derek and I, and four other guys. Do you need their names?"

Nate's body is tense, leaning toward Mark. In his mind he's already on to another question, "Eventually."

"We got into town and visited some of the bars, the top of the Space Needle, Starbuck's, you know all the touristy things." Mark shrugs. "We did some shopping, spent Friday afternoon fishing, the rest of the time we were at our hotel."

There it was. Nate circles around. "You went ... fishing?"

"We took out a charter that cleans the fish, so you don't have to touch them." Mark crinkles his nose. "We took the fillets back to the hotel and grilled fish tacos. May I have a glass of water?"

Pete is out of the office, Nate didn't listen to him when he left, so he's not sure where his partner went but it's up to Nate to take care of Mark's request. He hesitates, knowing that it will delay getting the information. He obligingly goes to the water cooler, fetches a paper cup, and fills it with water. On the way past Pete's desk, he grabs a box of tissue sitting on the corner and walks back to the distraught man sitting with shoulders hunched forward, his nose red and runny. Nate makes his voice very quiet, unconcerned. "Could you give me the name of the charter company you used?"

"I don't remember the name. We picked it

randomly out of the phone book. I didn't care which one we used, just so long as I didn't have to touch a fish. I've got the receipt at home. I can call you when I get back to my apartment and find it.

"Would it help if I gave you a phone book to look through."

"No, I wasn't really part of the selection committee."

Nate writes 'Fishing Charter?' on the pad of paper.

"Can you lead me up to the time Derek was no longer with you?"

"After the charter, we stayed around the pool. Derek, too. At least till around six or so. The other guys said he left to get a massage. He wasn't back by eight, so the rest of us went out for a movie and left him a message to call us. After the movie we stopped by a place for drinks. I kept texting him."

"No response?"

"No. I thought maybe he'd gone back to the room to lie down and had fallen asleep. We got back to the hotel around eleven. That was when I got the text."

"What was in the text?"

"I don't know the exact words, but it implied he never wanted to see me again." Mark's face crumbles.

"Do you still have the message?"

"No, I deleted it almost immediately."

"You were mad, I understand." Nate maintains a melodic tone.

"Derek and I go through this break-up dance about once a year. In the past, he'd be back within a couple weeks."

"So you had no reason to doubt this would be like any of the other times. What changed your mind?"

"Derek's mom," The words tumble out of Mark, like spilling a box of marbles. "She turned seventy-two on June sixth. Derek calls her every week, no matter what's going on in his life. And he never forgets a birthday no matter what or who he's doing. So when she called me to see if Derek was all right because he hadn't called her that started me worrying. I contacted Missing Persons right away—" His voice catches. "I never would have left Seattle if I thought he was in trouble." His eyes plead for Nate to believe him.

Nate ignores the snickers and murmurs of his fellow officers when Mark sobs openly, the tear-stained face in front of him his only concern. The phone conversation with his sister this morning comes back to him. Nate came out to his parents at fifteen. Nate's family was always close and gestures of affection were not uncommon so he envisioned a group hug and maybe a rainbow cake after dinner. Instead there were tears and silence. Deafening silence. Nate and his father haven't spoken since that day and it is perhaps that relationship that has Nate looking to Captain Bishop as a father figure. It took moving from Oklahoma to Washington and several years to pass for Nate to realize he's no less a person because of his sexual orientation and that he deserves the freedom to love anyone he chooses without coming under the judgment of others. Because of his experience with his family, he stays neutral at work focusing on the job. But it is getting harder to allow the hatred and prejudice to go unchecked.

"I really need the name of the fishing-charter

company you used. Is there anyone you could call to find out?"

Mark thinks a moment then pulls out his cell phone and picks a number. Nate waits as a connection is made and Mark quietly asks that person the question. Mark looks up at him, "Puget Sound Activity or something like that."

"Adventures?"

Mark repeats the word to the person on the other side of the phone call. He hangs up and looks at Nate. "Yes, Puget Sound Adventures."


*6:00 p.m.*

Last night John wore himself out worrying about the headaches and what they might mean to his ability to flashback and his general health. This led to analyzing how he felt about losing his super powers—sad, happy, worried, and disappointed. He always believed in being kind to others, putting others feelings before his, being the caregiver. Giving, always giving, and never putting himself in the front and center. When he was a child, he had a recurring dream in which he gathers up his family and friends, placing them in a large bubble that he carries on his back to fly away from dangerous monsters or a world on fire. As he grew older he realized the opportunities to save someone didn't come along in such a dramatic manner, however this new ability gave him a means to act if the need arose. Losing that ability will leave him dark and empty inside. That thought scares the hell out of him.

The cell phone on the table beside him lights up,

demanding his immediate attention. Save me. Save me. Save me. He saw *Nate Cliffton* in the person-calling-bar.

"Hey John, how would you like to hit the bars tonight?" Nate sounds excited, rushed, pushing the words out before him.

John is momentarily at a loss. "Tonight? Sure. I can't stay out late, I've got an early start tomorrow morning."

"Don't worry Cinderella, we'll get you home by midnight."

### 8:00 p.m.

John sits in a chair across from Nate sitting on the sofa. He tries to stop fidgeting, barely hanging on to an open-mind about the night ahead. He never thought of himself as homophobic, but he also never thought about pretending to be gay. "You want me to go to some local bars as your date?"

"Hey, you could do worse you know."

John thinks Nate really sounds hurt. That makes John more uncomfortable. Before he can take it back, Nate clarifies.

"You wouldn't really be my date, well not in the traditional sense, but you'll want to look like you only have eyes for me or you're going to get hit on right and left."

"Really? You think I'd be hit on?" All misgivings are gone replaced by a feeling of pride.

"In a heartbeat."

"Is this guy that we're retracing part of the

investigation you're working on?"

"My gut says yes. I don't think he disappeared on his own, for reasons the boyfriend presented. I thought if we go tonight there'll be a crowd and noises conducive to bringing on the right flashback."

"Conducive? What are you—my Psychic Enabler, now?" John laughs and grabs his keys, "I'm driving hot shot."

*10:30 p.m.*

John and Nate enter the Sea Unicorn at around ten-thirty—their third bar in a little over an hour, and so far the only thing that's occurred to John were several propositions and free drinks. This third location is a little seedier than the other two and not quite as noisy. John and Nate head over to the bar and sit.

"You want another beer," Nate asks him.

"I don't know, I'm feeling pretty wasted. Who knew all I had to do for free drinks was walk into a place and swing my ass a little."

Nate laughs and raises his fingers to the bartender to order two draft beers, "Maybe I'll get lucky tonight."

"Nope, sorry buddy, I'm taken body, heart, and soul by Ms. Susan Bishop," John sighs.

"This one serious?" Nate turns toward John, full attention.

"I think she's the one. Although she hasn't given me much of a chance so far. I'm still trying to work my charm. This is why I have to get up early tomorrow. I got myself invited to church with her and her dad."

"Wait, Bishop? Is she Frank's daughter?"

"Her dad's name is Steven, why?"

"Nothing. Just a coincidence."

The drafts arrive, and Nate raises his mug, looking at John with a broad smile. "Congratulations my friend, I wish you all the luck in the world."

John brings the mug up as well and touches Nate's glass before taking a drink; then he turns himself around on the swivel barstool and looks out at the crowd. One of the dancers gyrates, bends, and flips. *Whoa, I don't think I could move like that if my life depended on it* As he stares at the movements, he feels a sudden spike of pain on the right side of his head, and his vision blurs. Closing his eyes, he waits a beat to see if it goes away.

After a few seconds he opens his eyes. The music is different, the dancers that were just here seconds ago have changed, and the room is transformed, and noisy. He looks around at the bar, no Nate; John's adrenaline spikes. *Ok, this is it.* He looks around the room for Derek, trying to remember his features from the photo Nate had shown him. *He has auburn hair; that should stand out.*

It takes a few seconds, but John spots him. The auburn hair glows in the spotlights placed around the bar. Derek stands alone, dancing in place to the beat of the tune blaring out of the sound system. He isn't alone for long. A man with a martini glass in one hand and bottle of beer in the other joins him. Derek stops dancing and swoons against the man, picking up the drink. John's heart races. *Turn around,* he mutters, trying to see the man's face. Trim and powerful-looking, the man stands about five-feet-eight-

99

inches tall and is wearing a black t-shirt and jeans. His hair is sandy-colored and cut in a simple style. The man turns slightly to the right, and John gets a glimpse of high cheekbones before the man turns-away.

*If I move in closer I might see his entire face.* The thought propels him off the barstool. One step. Two. John is jostled hard enough to knock him back a step and pop him out of the flashback. "Excuse me." He mumbles, looking back through the crowd to where he last saw Derek and the mystery guy. They were gone, of course. Disappointed he turns back to the bar where Nate is and sits. So close. He was so close to seeing the man's face. This flashback thing was tricky. John updates Nate "I saw him. I saw him for just a moment, and then he was gone."

"You saw Derek? Was he with anyone?"

"Yes, he was with a man." John describes what he witnessed in the flashback. "I was trying to get closer to him when I ran into the Adam-Lambert-wannabe."

"Hey, that guy's kinda hot."

"Well, he should get his own look," John says.

"Why when this one is working so well for him? Don't sulk." Nate says.

"I'm not sulking. Let's stay here a while and see if it comes back to me." He wants to feel useful. Important. *The solver of murder cases.* "Let's move over to those high-tops."

They relocate and settle in to a round table built to surround a support beam covered with rope—very nautical. John begins a line of inquiry that has plagued him for some time. "You've seen me during a flashback. What does it look like from your end?"

Nate seems to be thinking carefully before replying. Finally, he says, "Well, let's talk about the Andra Hotel, for instance. At the hotel you seemed perfectly normal, but when you walked into the elevator car, you got real quiet. When we got to the ground floor, you stepped out. I knew you weren't with me, really. I mean physically you were, but you were in another world seeing things I couldn't. When you headed straight for that pond in the lobby I had to stop you, although you almost made that little girl's day."

John laughs. "What about just now?"

"You seemed fine, just sitting there staring out at the crowd, drinking your beer. You were quiet, but I knew you were attempting a flashback, so I just kept my mouth shut. Then, before I could stop you, you slid off the seat and right into the guy that was standing there big as day. That's when I knew you weren't here in my time."

John finishes his draft and puts the glass down. He shakes his head at the passing waiter to indicate he was done for the night.

"I always wondered what I looked like on the other end of a flashback. I thought I'd look like I was in a trance or a coma, so I'm always careful to stay in one place. It helps when you are with me, I can move around a little." John rubs his temple.

"Another headache?" Nate asks.

"Just started—it's got me thinking about losing what I have."

Nate grabs him around the shoulder and pulls him close.

"That's not the only reason I love ya, man."

101

John smiles wide and kisses his friend on the cheek, surprising the detective into letting him go.

"You know what I always thought?" John says. "I always thought when I went into a flashback that it was something like that Christopher Reeve movie; I'm going to have to look up the name of it, but the one where he goes back to … I'm not sure what time period. But he goes back because of a woman, and his body in the present goes into a coma, and he dies."

"*Somewhere In Time*."

"Yeah, but I'm not sure the time period."

"No, the name of the movie is *Somewhere In Time*, starring Christopher Reeve and Jane Seymour—the story of a young writer, who sacrifices his life in the present to find happiness in the past." Nate sheepishly repeats the movie spiel. "I cry at the end of the movie every time."

"That's it! That's what I think of when I'm under. Don't let them take me away in a coma, will you bro?"

John is assured by Nate that no one will take him anywhere.

"Do you have them when you're not with me? Of course you do," Nate answers his own question. "I guess I wondered how often you have them."

"About one a month; sometimes planned, other times not."

"Planned? So you think you are learning to control them?"

"Okay, I wouldn't go that far, but I'm having more luck getting to the right time period. You really cry every time you watch that movie? To this day if we watched it, you would cry?"

"To this day." Nate taps the tabletop. "Want to try it out? I've got Netflix. I'm sure we could find it in the classics."

"Hell, yes. It will give me ammunition I can use to tease cool, sophisticated Nate."

Nate cocks a thumb and waves it back and forth toward his chest. "Don't knock the power of the Reeve man."

## Chapter 19
### *June 9th – 11:30 a.m.*

John's hand is around Susan's as they stroll around the Pioneer Square district, in and out of pottery and antique shops off Main Street. Nate suggested taking Susan to the Police Museum, but John keeps that to himself, enjoying the quaint shops instead. Being with her is easy. She enjoys window-shopping and their casual conversation about the weather or the architecture of the buildings is pleasant. John finds out that Susan likes many of the same songs and they amuse each other by singing a few bars so the other can guess the name. John walks on a cloud next to Susan who glides along effortlessly, light brown hair falls loose to her shoulders and bounces as she coasts. A silver necklace compliments ivory skin and a mint-green dress with a tight bodice and full skirt shows off long, slender legs. John feels a tug of pride whenever he notices other men turn to stare.

The church service went well with John meeting many of Susan's friends. Afterward Susan's father drove home alone leaving his daughter to catch a ride home with John. The grin from ear-to-ear is permanent. *Stop it or she'll think you're not right in the head.* They walk the long front of a brick building. The panes of glass in the windows looked shimmery, as if wavy. A brass plaque beside the front door claims it as a historic site. John wonders what was housed here when it was first built. Blink.

Traffic sounds—horns blaring, engines roaring—are replaced by the jingle of horse carriages, the clop of hoofs. John inhales sharply the dust from the street. It puffs up from under wagon wheels and decorates the hems of the long skirts brushing the ground. A small group of people dressed in blankets and handmade capes and leather leggings walk on the opposite side of the street from John, proudly at attention. Panic sets in as he shakes his head hoping to come out of the flashback before Susan notices.

"John, you're hurting me." Her words pierce the quaint scene and brings him back to the now.

"Susan, I'm sorry. I didn't mean to hold on so tight."

"Are you okay?"

"Yes, just a little—, let's go inside here and get something to drink." John maneuvers her into a coffee shop and bookstore toward a table away from the window and a past just barely hidden from his view.


## 1:00 p.m.

Nate and Pete walk into the interrogation room where Captain Charlie Whitehead sits waiting to be questioned about a recent arrest for assault and battery. Nate knew this would likely lead nowhere. The charge was related to a fight between Whitehead and his brother over who would win the baseball game last weekend, Seattle or New York. The argument got loud and personal and arrests were made. But any reason to bring in personnel from Puget Sound Adventures makes Nate happy.

"Mr. Whitehead, or do you prefer Captain Whitehead?" Nate watches for a reaction to the title.

"Charlie's fine."

"Captain Charlie." Nate's voice rises in a lilt as if

he's just learned the name of his secret admirer. Whitehead frowns.

"Charlie," Nate begins again. "Do you know why you are here?"

The questions were light and interspersed with conversation, lulling Whitehead into a relaxed situation before narrowing to the subject Nate is most interested. Pete maintains his position in the corner as Nate takes a photo out of his folder and slides it across the table.

"Do you recognize her." Natalie smiles up at the men, sunglasses atop her head, green eyes shining bright.

"No. Should I?"

"How about these two." The second photo joins the first. In it Crystal and Chuck smile at the camera, arms linked.

Whitehead hesitates. His eyes slide to the left. He mumbles something and Nate leans forward. "Sorry Charlie, what did you say?"

"I said I might know these people."

"You pilot *The Mosquito*, correct?"

"Why is that important?"

"*The Mosquito*, not a very distinguished name. Not like *The Mariner*, all old man in the sea. Or *The Mermaid*, very King Titan. No, instead you've got *The Mosquito*, a pesky insect that passes on Malaria or Yellow Fever."

"No, you got it wrong. The name of the boat is a nod to the Puget Sound Mosquito Fleet."

"Mosquito Fleet?"

"You never heard of it," Whitehead's nose rose slightly and Nate knew he was going to be schooled.

"No, why don't you enlighten me."

"It was a collection of steamers and sternwheelers that plied the waterways from the early 1800s to the mid 1950s. I'm proud of my boat."

"Your boat, you mean Mr. Playford's boat."

"He's not the one sailing it every day now is he."

Nate wants to get back to Crystal and Chuck so he points at the photo and again asks Whitehead about them. Whitehead continues to dance around the answers, admitting they look familiar, not sure if they were on his boat, and unsure of his memory. Meanwhile his eyes look everywhere but at Nate's and he becomes sullen. Nate loses his temper, slamming his chair back against the wall as he stands.

"I don't believe you Charlie."

"Maybe I should think about getting a lawyer."

Nate shakes his head and looks at Pete. "I'll be back." He walks out of the room.


## 2:00 p.m.

Mr. Whitehead," Pete clears his throat and quietly speaks the man's name.

"You can call me Charlie." Pete's not the problem, the other one is the problem. Charlie wears a toothy grin.

"Mr. Whitehead, you understand that we are here to help. That the people in this photo have come to some harm."

"Harm, you mean—what do you mean?"

Pete slowly sits in the chair opposite Charlie. With an apologetic smile he explains, "They've both been murdered."

"Murdered! That's impossible. How could that happen?" Charlie pulls his hands back from the table and inches the chair back as if trying to get as far away from Pete as possible without leaving the room.

"What do you mean by that Mr. Whitehead?"

"Well, she—I mean they were so alive."

"You formed more of a relationship with Crystal than with Chuck?"

"Relationship? They were only on my boat once."

"I understand, but you seem closer to her."

Whitehead's eyes slide around the room and again he seems evasive, secretive. Pete's intuition kicks in.

"Mr. Whitehead, were you attracted to Crystal?"

### 3:00 p.m.

Nate stares at his computer screen where film from surveillance cameras show the street scene outside The Sea Unicorn. Nate is hoping to see Derek walking outside with the killer, the guy with high cheekbones that John saw. The black and white film shows people coming and going from the bar and Nate wishes for color to help him spot auburn hair. Only a few seconds later, he spies professionally coifed hair and imagines it's red as he looks at the face of Mr. Southwell who briefly looks toward the camera. Then Derek staggers and Nate sees that another man is there, hidden beneath the portico. The man steadies Derek and they both start toward the parking lot. Nate is sure this is their guy. *Turn around.* Nate hunches closer to the glass of the monitor and notes the time stamp, 10:10. The men turn the corner of the building and are out of sight.

Nate punches pause and hits the keys to bring up other camera feeds. Frustrated, he clenches his teeth, keeping the string of profanity in check. Finally he gets one that is at the rear of the Sea Unicorn's parking lot. The camera must be located on a light post at the back of the lot, facing the street and the back of the bar. Nate fast forwards to the correct time and seconds later the two men round the corner. *Turn around.* They head toward the right side of the computer screen, stumbling toward a dusty light-color vehicle parked under over-hanging trees that shadow that area of the lot. Nate tries to pierce the gloom with his human eye. One man, looks like Derek, slips to one knee before the other man gets him into the back seat of the vehicle. *Turn around.* The man turns. Flash. Then gone. One second of grainy black and white under the shadow of a tree. He picks up his phone and dials the Technology division for assistance.

Cavanaugh walks up, Nate looks at him then back down at the computer. "Did you release Whitehead?"

"Yes, I did." Pete continues to stand near him and Nate's curiosity overrides his desire to ignore the other man.

"And ..."

"Sir, I—"

"Don't call me sir."

Pete clears his throat, an annoying habit that Nate could do without, and begins again. "Charlie Whitehead and Ms. Knapp participated in carnal relations while she was aboard the fishing charter with her boyfriend Mr.

109

Connors."

"Holy shit. The boyfriend was right there?" That got his attention as Nate sat up straighter, all eyes on Pete.

"Apparently Mr. Connors paid quite a bit of attention to two young women who were aboard. Helping them with bait and casting the line. Ms. Knapp, left to her own devices, pursued her own kind of attention. With Mr. Whitehead."

"You let him go."

"That afternoon was the last he saw of them. He was very sorry to hear the fate that befell them ... her."

Nate looks at Cavanaugh, standing prim and fresh, unwrinkled. "And you believed him." A statement, not a question.

"Yes si—, yes. He gave me his exact steps on the day the two seem to have disappeared, complete with people who can swear he was with them. I contacted them before releasing him."

"Explains his twitchiness. Good job, Detective Cavanaugh." Nate's mouth clamps in a straight line as he begrudgingly compliments the young Englishman.

"Here are my notes if you would like to add them to your file, in your own words of course. For the record."

The man stood presenting his notepad to Nate as a peace offering. Nate feels a twinge in his chest. Like his heart is being jump-started. He warms as his face flushes. Nate motions for Pete to sit in the chair beside his desk. Then he points at the computer.

"I'm having IT work on this image. But it's our guy, Derek Southwell. And someone he's with the night of his disappearance."

110

Nate's phone rings and he picks up. Tom Bates interrupts him halfway through his greeting.

"Got some results for you; bad news for Detective Damone." Tom's voice is grim.

"Damone? He's over, where? Does he work out of the South Precinct?" Nate's heard the name.

"Yes. You know those body parts we recovered back in May? DNA just came back for the skull. It matches a woman, Michelle Kaiser."

"And that's where Damone comes in?" Absently Nate plays with a pile of "Bones" paperclips from a box that Tom gave him for Christmas.

"Yes. Two years ago she came up missing. Damone's the detective on it." There is rustling in the background as if Tom is leafing through paperwork.

"Have you contacted him?" Nate writes down the information and waits for Tom to finish.

"I just finished talking to him. Told him I was contacting you. He's expecting your call."


**4:00 p.m.**


"I'm Detective Cliffton and this is my partner, Detective Cavanaugh."

Nate is standing shoulder-to-shoulder with Pete in an office the size of a closet. His eyes slide over the surfaces in the cramped space taking in the piles of paper, the full wastebasket, and the rubber stress ball before resting on the swarthy features of a man squeezed into the space behind a desk, wondering if he crawled over or under

111

the desk to get there. The detective motions to two chairs wedged in front of the desk, just inside of the door. Nate and Pete take one step forward and sit.

"As you have heard from the Medical Examiner, we're investigating several murders and are involved in a missing person case. We uncovered remains that tie to one of your cases. Hope we can help each other."

"Detective Cliffton, it seems my missing person case has just become your homicide. I've contacted the family. They still had hope she would come home, so of course they're devastated. I pulled out my files on Michelle Kaiser when you called. I'd be happy to share my notes on the investigation with you. If you wish to take anything from this office, I must insist you sign on the dotted line." Damone indicated a Chain of Custody form on one corner of his desk.

"She went missing two years ago?"

"Almost three; I worked on it exclusively for a year before it hit the ongoing investigations pile."

"How'd you get DNA in the system?"

"The police found blood spatters on the ground by her vehicle in a parking lot near where she was last seen."

"And yet it was still being treated as a missing person?"

"There wasn't enough blood to indicate that death had occurred; could have been a bloody nose, a paper cut. Her purse and phone were missing, the car was locked, no witnesses. The suspects we questioned had alibis."

"How many suspects surfaced during the investigation?"

"We had two we were looking at hard—Michelle's

boyfriend and a guy who worked at a local fishing charter company."

There it is again. Fishing. A tic establishes itself under Nate's right eye.

"Michelle and her boyfriend were here on vacation. They went fishing the day before she disappeared. The guy on the boat was making a nuisance of himself, flirting, but not in a good way. Michelle and her boyfriend got in a fight about it the next night, the night she goes missing. Witnesses at the bar they were in confirmed some of the things they were yelling at each other."

"And the fishing charter; what was the name of the charter, and who did you question?" Nate leans forward, eager to hear the words

"Puget Sound Adventures."

*Yes.* "Who'd you have on the hook?"

"We talked to a Kessler. He was captain of the boat Michelle and her boyfriend went out on. Had an alibi for the night she disappeared."

"And I take it that alibi checked out. What about the boyfriend?"

"Bartender at the hotel they were staying, where they had the fight, poured him drinks most of the night. Had the front desk escort him to his room at around eleven. They swear he was too trashed to go after her. I checked the cameras in the lobby of the hotel. He never left. Raised holy hell about how we weren't doing our job that we were just out to get him. Stayed here in Seattle for an extra two weeks before giving up and heading home."

"Lovely fellow. Where was home?" Nate winks at Damone, cop-to-cop. *We've all seen the kind before. I'm*

113

*here for you.*

"Iowa. We checked his records. Nothing. And he passed the lie-detector test."

"Did you look into Puget Sound Adventures when you were interviewing Kessler?"

"No, didn't think it was necessary."

"We keep coming up with the name. Nothing concrete, just a pattern of coincidences."

"I hate coincidences," the thick-browed Damone mutters.

"Tell me about it. The Captain won't let me go after a warrant for the entire company unless I have something solid, doesn't want to upset the tourist industry. So I keep picking around the edges, looking at their computers, bringing their employees in and questioning them," Nate turns to look at Pete. "Let's get Playford in."

"Gotta keep our politicians happy. Good luck," Damone stands and leans forward to grab Nate's hand in both of his. Nate is pleasantly surprised at the dry warmth of the grip.

"Yeah, I'm going to need it."

## Chapter 20

*June 12<sup>th</sup> – 10:00 a.m.*

Willis Playford III sits in a chair across from Nate in a conference room a little cleaner than the interrogation rooms. Pete stands in the corner, hands folded in front of him. Nate watches the other man settle in before speaking.

"Mr. Playford, I appreciate you coming in to talk to me."

"My pleasure Detective Cliffton. Anything I can do to help."

"Your company, Puget Sound Adventures is a place of interest in a murder investigation—"

"What do you mean? Why has no one come to me about this?"

Nate holds up his right hand, palm out, "Mr. Playford, please understand PSA is in no way implicated and you are not in trouble. I've had some of your employees in for questioning and now I want to ask you a few questions about your staff."

"Is anyone in trouble?"

"No."

"Okay, very well." Playford's eyes are bright and have a disconcerting way of staring straight through Nate. He doesn't like Playford.

"Could you tell me a little something about your hiring practices?"

"Like what?"

"Background checks, any reason to fire anyone lately?"

Playford stays cool and calm, answering all the

questions and deflecting the background checks and management of personnel to Darius Adamya.

"Adamya, I didn't think he had so much power."

"Darius is a smart man with a lot of knowledge about the service PSA provides. I trust his judgment completely."

"Well several of your customers, visitors to the area, they don't seem to make it out of Seattle."

"What do you mean by that?"

"They have a way of dying within two days of buying a four-hour fishing tour through your company."

A reaction, any reaction, but the guy's either too smart or smooth or doesn't give a shit about people dying. Nate gets nothing from him. Playford fends off several more questions before hinting at his attorney. Nate wraps up.

"Thank you for talking to me and helping me to understand the running of one of your businesses. If I have further questions, may I contact you?"

"You can try, but I'm usually not so accommodating. Your best bet would be to contact Darius or my attorney."

The slam is not wasted on Nate and it takes all his discipline to continue smiling. *Note to self, get Adamya in here.* Playford turns to Nate before leaving through the door, "Or, contact your Chief of Police, ask him to get a hold of me, he's got my private number."


*1:00 p.m.*


116

John walks around the patterned side chair where Brandy sits facing a sofa, two chairs, and two end tables covered with year-old magazines. The Radiology waiting room, with a fish tank and a hutch where a pot of coffee and hot water for tea or cocoa sits, is designed to put the patients at ease. The effect is lost on John who paces around the space. There's only one other person in the room besides the siblings, so John doesn't keep his voice down.

"What's taking them so long?"

"Oh for crying out loud, sit down and relax. See how calm I am?" Brandy doesn't look up when she speaks to him.

"You're playing Sims on your cell phone; you're transferring your anxiety to the characters on the screen."

"Mr. Carpenter," calls out one of the registered nurses behind the long reception desk. John hurries to the counter with Brandy on his heels.

"Mr. Carpenter, we've seen something on this latest CAT scan that concerns us, and we would like to explore it further."

This is it, that worry he kept saying was nothing was really something. "OK, shall I make another appointment?"

"You are to report to the reception area in the emergency room of our facility; everything will be explained to you there." She is polite but dismissive. Cutting off any disagreement or questions.

John ignores her tone. "What needs explaining? Don't I just need to schedule an appointment?" His voice tightens and rises.

"Please, continue down the hall, follow the gold

arrows on the tile to the Emergency Room, and give the person at the reception desk this envelope. They will set up the next steps you'll have to take." The nurse hands over a large manila envelope and turns away from him. She picks up someone else's file.

Too stunned to ask further questions, John turns and with Brandy heads in the direction of the arrows pointing to the ER. In the reception area, John gives the envelope to the busy attendant and repeats what the nurse in Radiology told him, thinking that all would be clear to this woman. However, she doesn't seem to know what to do with him either, but takes the envelope and politely asks them both to sit in the waiting area while she finds out what is to happen next. John and Brandy sit among people complaining because they have been here for hours and haven't been called. John rolls his eyes at Brandy.

An hour later they are paged and directed to a small consultation room connecting to the emergency reception area. They sit opposite a woman who holds a manila envelope containing, John presumes, the results of his CAT scan. She has a pleasant face. Round with oval glasses and white, wispy hair. She has added homey touches to an otherwise sterile office—portraits of her grandchildren, a plant, and a hand-crocheted afghan over the back of her chair. "Mr. Carpenter, we're going to send you to Harborview for another test. Did they explain that to you?"

John feels both numb and emotional, as if he is frozen, but at the least amount of urging could break down and cry. "No, not really."

"It looks like you are to report for an MRI. There's some concern with the results of your most recent CAT scan and a more thorough test may provide the answers. An MRI produces a more detailed scan than the one here at our facility."

"What exactly does M-R-I stand for?

"Magnetic resonance imaging, the cameras take the x-rays at shorter intervals and the image is clearer."

"Do I set up the appointment with you? My sister and I can just drive over there."

"I'm sorry, Mr. Carpenter, but we're legally required to transport you via ambulance to the other facility as we haven't officially released you from our care."

She collects insurance information from John and then asks them to again sit in the waiting area, assures them that his name will be called, and an emergency-room bed will be provided where he will see a doctor before being transported to the hospital.

"This was just supposed to be a routine test." John sits back down in the reception area to stare at nothing in front of him. Another hour passes before he's called. He rises and looks over at a couple with a sick child who have been waiting since before he got to the Emergency Room.

"I must be in really bad shape if they are calling me before them."

Brandy shushes him and pushes on his back, so he starts moving to a curtained cubicle where he's shown to a bed. A male nurse takes his blood pressure and asks, "Do you know why you're here?"

"It's not entirely clear," John says.

"No? Well, I'll go find your records and see if I can get some answers for you. They are a little busy right now, but you shouldn't have to wait not knowing why you're here."

"Thank you, I'd appreciate that." Brandy reaches for John's hand, and he squeezes it and smiles at her. "I guess the headaches were a little more serious than I thought."


*3:30 p.m.*

The nurse returns.

"Well, it appears you have what is classified as a meningioma. It's a mass on the right side of your skull. Because of where it's located, the size and shape of it, I'm 99% sure it's benign, but they will have to do the MRI to be sure, which is the reason they sent you down here. Your paperwork is being processed, and we've contacted an ambulance for you, so it shouldn't be long now. Has a doctor been in to see you?"

"No." John doesn't want to go back into a hospital. That's what being in a hospital for three plus weeks will do for you. He sits thinking of his options. "My sister is with me, and we're parked right out front. She could drive me over to Harborview, save you guys the effort."

"You stay put. Once you've checked in, you can never leave." He winks at John. "I'll check on the doctor." Then he finishes with the blood pressure pump, flips the tubing over his head, wraps the cuff around his neck, and leaves the same way he came in.

The doctor comes in next and the first question out of his mouth is, "Do you know why you are here?"

John thinks it's a bit redundant, but replies, "I'm

120

still a little in the dark."

"Mr. Carpenter, the routine CAT scan shows you have a growth, something that's called a meningioma, on the right side of your skull. Where it's located and the shape of it—it's mostly round. This one looks benign. We won't know for sure until the MRI. Have you had any feelings of pressure or headaches?"

"A few," John answers sheepishly. "I was going to talk to a doctor about them when my CAT scan results came back, but I never got the chance."

"Any blurred vision."

He thinks of the flashbacks. "Nothing that I've noticed so far, but I have had some dizziness."

"We're sending you to Harborview for the MRI. Their equipment is more precise than what is available at this facility."

John makes one last ditch effort to regain control. "I was told my sister and I couldn't drive over there."

"That's right, Mr. Carpenter, you'll be transmitted in an ambulance."

John is quiet while the Emergency Room doctor delivers the news, and then he brightens. "Will there be sirens?"


*4:30 p.m.*


Nate and Pete sit in straight-back chairs in front of a massive desk. Captain Bishop is balanced, leaning back in his padded chair and Lieutenant Gale, Nate's section leader, sits in a side chair with arms to the right of the desk

121

facing Nate who looks down at the notes in his lap. Pete had carefully typed a chronological record of their investigation—double-spaced with clarifying Post-it notes in the margins.

"Nate we've heard from the DA's office that you questioned Willis Playford. You do know who Willis Playford is?"

The tone of voice puts Nate on edge but he only says, "Yessir."

"Did you also know that he has a standing tee time with the mayor every third Saturday of the month, flies up here in his private Cessna for a day. Foursome sometimes includes our police commander and Congressman Mumford Edward Hurlburton III, an up and comer in Seattle."

The question beats him down and all Nate can do is provide a weak excuse.

"I wanted to talk to him about his employees, not about him personally, and give him an update on the investigation."

Bishop holds up his hand to stop him, Nate sits trying to keep his knee from jerking.

"What have you got so far?"

"Natalie Sullivan, Crystal Knapp, and Chuck Connors were visitors to Seattle. Murdered, presumably at sea where their body or body parts were found. The women had traces of Thorazine in their tissues; I'm still waiting for the results on the man. All three were disfigured in the same way—right ear missing." Nate recites.

"Thorazine? Have you determined that this drug was used to subdue the victims?" Captain Bishop frowns.

"Yes. After talking to family and friends neither woman appears to have had a prescription. Tom Bates, the Forensic Pathologist, confirmed that Thorazine when used in large quantities can be a sedative."

"And the disfiguring," Lieutenant Gale inquires.

"Same type blade used on the wounds." Nate looks back to his notes before continuing. "There's another missing person, Derek Southwell, also a visitor to Seattle who went fishing on a PSA charter." This last is said apologetically since Nate has to bring up Playford's business once again. He clears his throat, "I have reason to tie this person to our case."

"What led you to that conclusion?" Captain Bishop's face is stone and Nate cannot read what he's really thinking. Nate's scalp feels hot and itchy.

"Besides the fishing charter, text messages sent over the phone of the missing person is suspicious as is the text sent by the first victim's phone. We are treating his disappearance with suspicion"

Captain Bishop wrinkles his nose and turns to Lieutenant Gale. "Nasty business." Then turning to Nate, "You get the worst cases. It's like you're a macabre magnet."

Nate giggles, not sure how to take the statement.

"You've been through PSA's records. They've been cooperating with the investigation." The Captain says this as if to dismiss the company.

"Yes, but—"

"But what Detective?"

Nate looks at Bishop, tongue-tied. Then he sees Pete's post-it note regarding Damone's case.

123

"Another woman, Michelle Kaiser, who went missing three years ago showed up dead with ties to our case as well as Puget Sound Adventures. Medical examiner says the mutilation on the right side of her head is consistent with what we've seen. We talked to the officer assigned back in 2010 and working her case. Detective Damone informed us that Ms. Kaiser went out on a fishing charter before disappearing.

"Have you run a search of the database to see if there are anymore older cases?" Gale asks. *Obvious question.* "Yeah, Pete's still running it; every bit of new information goes in."

Nate doesn't look at Pete as he answers for him. "IT is looking at security tapes obtained from a local bar to see if we can get a better picture of the men leaving it. One of them is Derek Southwell."

"You seem fixated with PSA and yet besides the coincidence of it being a popular tourist destination for fishing our great waters, you have nothing to tie the murders to the employees or the owner."

Nate feels as if Bishop is accusing him of something. The man Nate always viewed as a father figure is sounding like a stranger. In the name of self-preservation, Nate thought about pointing at Pete and blaming him for the direction the case was headed. Nate carefully walks through the minefield of emotions. "Captain, the link to PSA is there in each one of the victims folders."

"Does PSA share its client list with any other businesses in the area?" Lieutenant Gale calmly asks.

"Not according to the manager there." Nate's voice

is louder than he intends.

"Having the same company surface in each of the cases raises our level of interest, of course; Nate, talk to the District Attorney's office, and see if that's compelling-reason enough to constitute a warrant to search the boats and warehouse, which is what I'm assuming you want to do." Lieutenant Gale says.

"I can do that sir. Also Detective Cavanaugh and I are using available public information to check the online activities of PSA's employees, and we're running their names through the criminal database."

"Someone could be making it look like PSA or someone that works there is responsible, pointing a finger for some reason," Bishop says.

"It's possible, but why?"

"It might be worth it to you to find out."

The statement from Bishop is like a blow and Nate flinches.


### 5:30 p.m.

Heading back towards their desks, Nate turns to hand the folder over to Pete. "I'm going out for a while. I want to swing by the parking lot where Michelle Kaiser's car was found. Get Kominski's help on anything if you need it. I don't think he's caught a case yet. I'll be back in a few."

"Oh yeah, me and Kominski are getting along so well." The sarcasm is not lost on Nate but right now he doesn't care. The meeting with Bishop left him feeling further away from solving the case. As if his focus on PSA is completely unfounded and his only reason for doing it is to dismantle the entire Seattle PD and high-placed public officials. *I need to get out. Run. Run. Run away.*


## 5:30 p.m. (across town)

*I can't do this. I'm outta here. Run. Run. Run away.*

John bolts out of bed; panic over the upcoming mutilation of his brain has made its way from said brain to his heart. The speed at which the latter is now beating propels him up and out, slipping when his stocking feet hit the linoleum floor. He reaches for the tote bag containing his personal belongings from the small cabinet that serves as a closet. He shrugs out of his gown and pulls on the jeans he wore into the hospital. His shirt hangs open as he laces up a sneaker on his right foot. Turning to the left shoe something catches his eye, and he looks up and freezes.

"Going somewhere?" Susan leans against the corner of his bed, watching him with wide eyes but the tone of her voice belies the innocence of those deep, brown orbs. "I thought you had a date with a surgeon later this morning?"

*Great. Caught.* Guilt flushes his cheeks and tangles up his vocal cords. "Hey there, you surprised me. I didn't expect you."

"So, there will be a surgical procedure?" Spoken like a mom.

He watches her slowly circle the end of the bed.

"Yeah, MRI's scheduled for tomorrow." He looks down at his disheveled attire before meeting her eyes and exhaling loudly. "I'm starving." It seems like the most

126

logical thing to say.

"Wasting away, you poor thing. So you were going out for doughnuts?" She smiles at him, encouraging the white lie.

"Yeah, I guess," he mumbles. Then his shoulders rise up in a shrug. "I guess I'm a little worried."

"That's understandable. Do they have to shave your head?"

John frowns, trying to find the answer to her question. Up until now he hasn't thought too much about the process, only about the possibility of losing the flashbacks. "I—I don't know." He watches her settle on the bed across from where he is still sitting in the side chair near the window. "I'm a little worried that I might lose something after the surgery."

Concern floods her eyes and she quietly asks, "Mobility or cognitive issues?" Her hand starts to reach toward his knee but stops.

"No, nothing like that." He wriggles around trying to get comfortable before deciding it would take more than moving into the right position. He'd feel more comfortable at home. He takes a deep breath and continues, chooses his words carefully.

"You know about the coma I was in last year."

She nods and the way she is leaning in and holding his gaze, she is obviously trying to flirt him out of his fear.

"What I didn't tell you is what happened to me when I got out of the hospital." The words march out of his mouth one slow step after another, like a doomed man marching to his fate. "I seem to have acquired a special ability."

"You can see through walls?" She tips her head sideways and grins at him. "Or you wear your underwear on the outside and fly?"

"Okay, so not that special." He frowns. He doesn't want to laugh right now. "I seem to be able to see into the past."

"Into the past?" The hand that is reaching out returns to her lap. Her back straightens as she looks at him.

He can see doubt flicker in her eyes so he quickly tries to explain his statement. "Have you ever wanted to see what a house looked when it was first built, what the neighborhood looked like, why the house was angled the way it was?"

The doubt is no longer flickering but taken hold. John rushes on, "Well, I've *always* wanted to do that, and now I can. You're freaked out aren't you?"

"I—" Susan looks around as if she's lost something, fingers plucking at her skirt. "I have to go." She is up and out of the room faster than John can react. The room is empty and he's sitting in a chair surrounded by windowed-walls and curtained-dividers. *Shit.*

# Chapter 21
*June 13<sup>th</sup> – 9:00 a.m.*

Two days in the hospital seems like two weeks. John is wheeled through the door of his room after the MRI to find his mom and a garish bouquet of balloons and ribbons.

"Aw, Mother, you shouldn't have. I don't think I'll be in here long, not like the last time."

"I thought you could use a little color." Cheerful, yet dismissive, she looks only at the arrangement.

"It's certainly colorful." John gives her a hug before climbing back into bed, contemplating when would be a good time to pass it along to someone else on the floor. Light from the windows shines in his eyes and his mother rises from the visitors chair to remedy that. Half-turned to him, she asks, "So, what have they told you so far?"

"The MRI will help them see what they're dealing with. I should know later this afternoon or by tomorrow morning if I'm going in for surgery."

"I talked to Susan."

"Oh, really?" John is cautious, wondering if Susan confided in his mom that he was crazy.

"She's worried about you, but I told her you'll be fine. Just a little surgery."

"Hey, could you contact Nate?" John changes the subject. "Just let him know I'll be off-line for a couple days."

"No worries, I'll call him as soon as I get home. So how is it going with you and Susan?"

John's eyes slide to the left; he knew that question wasn't far behind.

## 11:00 a.m.

His mother left to start getting a meal around, so that it was on the table when his dad got home for lunch. His dad hadn't missed a lunch at home in all the years John lived there. It didn't seem to matter the weather, traffic, or his workload, somehow he always walked through the back door and right up to the dinette table for his mid-day meal. They would both be back later. John was to call them if he found out the time of surgery.

Chewing on his lower lip John mulls around the prospect of surgery. He wonders for the zillionth time if the flashbacks will still be with him. He rather enjoys the glimpses into the past. A few are scary, but for the most part they are fun and beautiful shots of history. He rolls over on his side and tries to relax, fluffing the pillow under his head. He always wanted to be looking at a modern-day scene and be able to blink and open his eyes to the same scene ten, twenty, fifty, or one hundred years earlier. The flashbacks gave him that ability. He's sullen at the thought of losing the special attribute.

*If I no longer have flashbacks, I'm back to normal, and that's good, right?*

Daydream-Susan pops up waving a hand so his thoughts pay attention to her. When he thinks of Susan his stomach flutters. The way he feels about her is good and scary at the same time, almost like the flashbacks. And now he's scared her away with his revelation. His thoughts materialize into the real Susan who marches in the door

130

past the nurse who just delivered to John a pill to keep his sugar down or his blood coagulation up. He's lost track and resolves to just get the whole thing over. Her mouth is set in a thin line. She looks like someone who lost an argument and is paying up. John holds his breath trying to read her face.

"Prove it. Do it right now. Go into the past and tell me what you see." She looks like a younger version of herself, frustrated with a magician at her childhood birthday party.

"I ... I ..." John's brain is filled with sawdust and nothing is functioning. He spreads his hands to show her he has nothing up his sleeves.

"Tell me what you see while sitting in this room."

Now the last time John was in Harborview he had a flashback showing a meat packing warehouse. An industry that fizzled out to be torn down, leveled, and rise, like a Phoenix to become King County hospital in the late 1920s. In 1931 it was dedicated as Harborview. He's feeling pressure to perform and those are not conditions conducive to a flashback. John remembers his conversation with Nate the other night.

He closes his mouth and his brain starts working again. "Susan, sit. Please."

She moves closer, hesitates, and then settles down on the bed beside him.

"I would understand if you no longer wanted to be my girlfriend. I wouldn't like it, but I would understand." He's talking faster. "I didn't mean to scare you. I was hoping it would be something I could share with you. I'm not an axe-murderer. The flashbacks don't interfere with

131

my job ..." It registers that she is smiling. *That's a good thing, right?*

All the muscles in her face soften. "You called me your girlfriend."

"That's what you got? Out of everything I've just said that's what you heard?"

Susan touches her fingers to John's lips to shush the words.

"Well, apparently you cannot flash ... back? Cute word; so you cannot flashback on demand and you are afraid that after the surgery today, you'll no longer have the ability to flashback when you want? And that would upset you?" She says it simply and calmly, and John can only nod in astonishment.

"Well, there's not much you can do now since this surgery is going on as planned. After all, your health is the most important thing here."

"You are the most important thing, er, person here." He's desperate to be with her. John and Susan against the world.

She smiles and says. "You'll just have to see what happens after surgery."

John is confused. Does she mean he will have to wait until after surgery to see if he still has his ability? Or will Susan know better after surgery whether or not she'll stay. He's afraid to ask for fear of getting an answer he doesn't like so he gulps it all down and simply smiles.

"My family doesn't know anything about the flashbacks. Please don't say anything."

"I promise not to tell."

"So you're not afraid of me?" He dares to ask this

one question.

"I think seeing into the past is romantic." She reaches for his hand and he is grateful for this small gesture.


## 1:00 p.m.

Nate appears around the cloth room divider with a bag of Doritos and a six-pack of cola.

"Nate, ol' buddy, you know how to pick out gifts."

The balloon bouquet to relegated to the floor to clear his tray for Nate's offering.

"Mom get hold of you?"

"Good thing too. I was going to put out an APB for my psychic investigator. I've been calling.

"Brandy's got my phone." The pained look on John's face says it all.

John explains to Nate about the meningioma and the looming. Nate tells him about his new partner. This piece of information seems to be at the top of Nate's list of important things that have happened to him lately.

John studies his friend to see the effects of the new work arrangement. Nate seems tense, nerves humming, movements brisk. But then one of the doctors taking care of John walks in and Nate transforms into a smooth, calm lion watching his prey.

"He's cute," Nate murmurs after the young doctor leaves the room.

John rolls his eyes, smiling. "So, where is this partner of yours?"

Nate waves his hand past his eyes, like he's shooing a fly. "I left him at the office. I needed to come see you." The brilliant smile flickers but John sees the gentleness in his eyes.

"Well, I know you don't really like to share your toys, but if he can help you, keep you safe, I'm all for it."

"Yeah, well, you're not right in the head. We've got X-rays and doctors to prove it."

## Chapter 22 – More Reflections of a Killer

Wiping a soft cloth around in circles on the chrome fixtures of the boat is one of my least-fatal distractions. Sounds of seagulls flavor the background and the aromatic scent of the marina fills my nostrils. The morning air around me is wet, but no rain falls.

Its different here than other places I've visited in the name of dad's ambition. In Michigan the wetness had a scent of mold and earth and growing things. In Florida the air was sharp, like the inside of an empty shell when you hold it to your nose, tangy with the odor of ancient dead things. In Georgia, the smells were verdant from the abundant plant-life and high temperatures over the lowlands.

Before I finished college, my parents moved back to Washington. When I finished college I stayed away. Away from the watchful eyes of doctors and accusatory stares of parents. I traveled a lot getting jobs where I could find them, never wanting to settle.

When my mom passed in 2002 of ovarian cancer, I didn't go home. My dad passed a year later of a heart attack, I still didn't go home. I continued visiting doctors and refilling the Thorazine, collecting the pills in a ceramic jar that said *Bucket List* on the front. I stayed under the radar, honing my craft, keeping ahead of the law. Michigan, Florida, and Georgia were my training grounds. Then I returned home.

Chapter 23
*June 15<sup>th</sup> - 11:30 a.m.*

Brain surgery salad. John thinks of the studio album by Emerson, Lake, and Palmer that is hidden in his classic rock collection. John came out on the other end of surgery in one piece, now the waiting game. The wait to see if he still has the flashback ability.

Lying on a chaise lounge on the patio lovingly built by his father when John was young, he is surrounded by the scent of his mother's favorite annuals planted in the wooden boxes around the outer edge of the concrete slab. He closes his eyes. The sound of a good-natured argument floats toward him from the open kitchen window. It's about the right way to fold napkins and whether or not to serve tea or lemonade, or go with his dad's choice, beer.

The recuperation plan John has in mind this time is to stay here the rest of the weekend and then head back to his apartment to spend the rest of his sick leave out from under the watchful eye of his mother.

He must have dozed because children's laughter brings him out of a light nap. Looking around, he wonders whose kids are here. A girl of about seven darts out from under the lilac bushes along the back of the yard and skips over to a younger version of John. He chortles in triumph at the realization that he's flashed back to a moment in time when he is around twelve, and he and Brandy are playing a version of cops and robbers. Only in this version he is the sheriff/librarian and his sister is the outlaw. Somehow he always included librarian duties in any of their role playing. John watches his younger self sit at a makeshift table, pretending to stamp books with what looks like a wooden block. Brandy is crouched, a banana in one hand like a revolver and a pillow case in the other. She tiptoes toward him. Just as she gets ready to jump onto the patio, she lets out a loud fart. *Braackk!* The children look at each other, stunned. Then gales of laughter at her surprisingly loud body function interrupts the mood and the game is over.

"Here we go." His mother's voice startles him and he comes all the way out of the flashback to see her walk into his line of vision with a tray of food. She places it on a table set for the occasion, followed by his father with another tray of food.

"Hope you're hungry," Dad says. "Your mother made enough to feed the neighbors."

John looks back toward where the children were playing, replaced now by a planter of flowers and a chaise similar to the one he is in. He stands and walks toward his folks, who are fussing over the table. Feeling incredibly lucky to be through with the surgery and blessed to still have his flashbacks, John crows, "I could eat an adult elephant and his horse."

## Chapter 24 – Final Reflections of a Killer

My dad always told us kids—*You need focus. Focus on the ball. Focus on your teacher. Focus on becoming a man we can be proud of.* Okay so this last one wasn't for my sisters, it was directed at me—right between the eyes. And no matter that I usually ignored him I guess the nut doesn't fall far from the tree because my focus sharpened about three years ago.

Before 2010, I focused on the homeless or someone down on their luck—a hapless wanderer or streetwalker. People no one would miss or spend too much time or effort seeking. The thrill of the kill was there, but it grew tedious, not challenging. I was sitting in a bar drinking a beer and watching other people doing the same thing. The sound was turned down low on the television nearest me. I didn't care, didn't need to hear the chatter, just watch the pictures. I perked up when a news story came on about the murder of a local woman, Dorothy Fremont, a bartender at The Willatuk. I knew Dorothy. Had spent many nights at The Willatuk—good deep-fried pickles. Dorothy was the kind of bartender that made you feel as if you were home, sitting around chit-chatting and quaffing a beer. Like Miss Kitty on the old Gunsmoke series—a whore with a heart of gold. Miss Dorothy met her fate one night after her shift at the bar. She was raped and stabbed—or stabbed, then raped—in an empty lot near her home. The news reporter assured the public that the police got their man; a guy from Arizona was arrested at the Seattle-Tacoma International Airport.

For some reason I found this story truly inspiring and morbidly fascinating. It was on that night in 2010 a

138

seed was planted. One that germinated and grew and blossomed into the conviction that now was as good a time as any to focus. I could hear my dad's voice in my ear, gravelly insistence. *Focus on the goal. Focus on opportunity.* Focus on tourists. Focus on killing one visitor at a time.

## Chapter 25
*June 17<sup>th</sup> – 8:00 a.m.*

Footsteps. Nate waits a few more steps before looking up to see Pete continue towards him with a take-out container of caffeine and a question, "Have you been here all night?"

"What time is it?" Nate reaches for the coffee.

"Eight a.m."

"Then I've been here all night."

"Good God, man. You should have called, I'd have come in."

Nate stands and stretches. "No reason both of us should lose sleep.

"Find anything." Pete doesn't sound hopeful.

"Pete, I started looking at the case, trying to come at it from another angle, stir things up. We've got three dead people, four if we add Michelle, and five if we give up on Derek and include him in the lot."

"True." Pete nods and remains standing near Nate.

"We got no fingerprints, no weapon, not much to go on."

"Except all our victims used PSA."

"No, no, let's not go there." Nate holds his hands up as if surrendering. "And we're still waiting on IT to send us the photo, but I don't have much faith they'll be able to clean it up. Have you heard anything from them?"

"Only that they tried to enlarge the image without much success and were using a new process to try again."

Nate nods, dismissing IT. "So I started going through past cases involving visitors to Seattle."

"Oh." Pete's eyebrows arch upward.

"I found quite a few cases, one or two still open, so I start looking through the files to find similarities, anything that ties to ours, you know, taking PSA out of the equation, leave our options open so we don't miss anything or anyone. And you know what?"

Pete's face is response enough as his eyebrows crawl even higher on his forehead. Nate has his partner's full attention so he draws out his words, slow like an unveiling. "Drum roll please." He bends over and actually does a drum roll on his desk top. "Who do you think I found in one of the older cases?" Nate doesn't wait for a response, "Charlie Whitehead, captain of the fishing charter the killer took out the day Dorothy died." Nate places his hands on a dusty box on the right side of his desk and continues. "I just keep coming back to PSA no matter how I look at this case.

Pete nods towards Nate's ruined jacket, "Tom Ford, not exactly the brand to wear in your line of work."

Nate ignores the jab and flicks his hand down the front of the jacket to remove a thin smear of dirt and sits back down in his chair and takes a sip of coffee, grimacing before swallowing. *Too much Hazelnut.* "This is the entire record of evidence, trial documents, and conviction papers for the investigation into the murder of Ms. Dorothy Fremont."

"And Mr. Whitehead's name is in there somewhere."

Nate nods before changing direction. "Did you get a chance to look at the security tapes Damone gave us?"

"Of course. You ask, I deliver."

Still with the sarcasm. Nate rolls his eyes, "And?"

"Nothing showing the parking lot where Ms. Kaiser's car was found."

Nate shakes his head in frustration and points at the box. "Most of the notes in the file are from a Detective Reagan. He brought Charlie in and held him for twenty-four hours. A woman, Florence Samples, stepped forward with an alibi so they released him. Hours later they arrested some guy at the airport."

Pete smirks, "Just like on telly." Then he gets serious, "Mr. Whitehead seems to pop-up everywhere."

"Hey, he's your friend."

"He opened up to me because I got him to focus on helping us."

"You're such a good detective." Nate's lip curls in a sneer, belying the compliment.

Pete's face settles into a sad, puppy-dog expression, "It's probably the British accent."

Nate cannot help himself. He throws his head back, hitting it on the chair, and laughs loudly. After the first blast, choking back tears and the next wave of laughter, he recovers. "Cavanaugh, I may be getting used to having you around. We've talked to Charlie. Before we bring him in again, let's go see good ol' Flo."

*10:00 a.m.*

Nate and Pete pull up in front of an older home. One of those that started out life as an abode to a family of ten— wall-to-wall kids and granma and granpa housed on the first floor. Over the years many renovations have taken place and the structure now serves as apartments. Florence Samples is on the ground floor, if apartment 110 is any indication. They walk up the narrow sidewalk, past a patchy lawn and a four-foot creepy angel statue with head bowed and both hands over the eyes. Nate keeps his eyes on the coy figure. *Don't blink,* his inner-Whovian whispers. He rings the doorbell and they wait only a few seconds before the door opens and Flo bursts out as if she's expecting them.

"I'm Detective Nate Cliffton, this is my partner Detective Cavanaugh, and we'd like to ask you a few questions."

"Honey, you can ask me any little 'ol thing you want, you lookin' as good as you look." Flo's seen better days with hair that's been bleached so many times it looks like cotton candy and make-up that looks shoveled on a few years back and clinging like a scab that refuses to completely let go. Clumps of mascara threaten to drop on the lounge-set she's wearing. Nate decides she wears the chiffon outfit to bed as well as to the local grocer's or to pay her parking tickets. The pink ruffle around the sleeves shows signs of wear. She opens the door wider so the two men can enter. A swell of cat urine rolls toward Nate who instinctively snaps his nostrils shut and walks in with Pete behind him. They follow another aroma that temporarily masks the cat—that of musk and cigarettes that drifts off Flo.

She glides toward a chair in her pink living room. She's almost there when the smooth motion is ruined by an overweight Tabby who wraps itself around her ankles. She stumbles but grabs a floor lamp to steady herself never losing her grip on the cigarette.

"Danny Boy!" She scolds the cat who, undaunted, looks up and blinks. Flo points to a settee for Nate and Pete. They carefully settle among the feather and downy pillows with pink ruffles.

"Ms. Samples, are you still in touch with Charlie Whitehead?"

"Who?" Her eyelashes flutter and Nate watches a black flake of mascara drop to her cheek.

"Charlie Whitehead, you were his alibi a few years back."

"Oh, yes Charlie. No I haven't seen him in a couple years." Her shoulders squeeze together, dismissing Charlie and setting her ample bosom to jiggling. *J-E-L-L-O.*

"The alibi you provided released him from a murder investigation." Nate sees panic flicker in her eyes but the cat gives her a distraction when he climbs up into her lap and starts purring. She pets Danny Boy with one hand and flicks the tip of her cigarette into a pink ceramic ashtray with the other. "Well, honey, that was so many years ago. How y'all think I'm going to remember."

"Ms. Samples, you stated that Charlie took you to dinner on the night in question. Then you both came back to your place for the remainder of the evening. Is that true?" An edge creeps into Nate's voice as he feels himself losing patience.

"Is Charlie in trouble again? Well if that's what I said, then it's true."

"Ms. Samples—"

"Call me Flo. Pu-leese." She slowly eyes Nate going from his feet crossed at the ankle to his chest where

144

she stops her perusal. "Detective Cliffton I'll bet you turn all the girls' heads."

*I need to shower.* Nate doesn't mind flirting. In fact some of his favorite conversations involve naughty dialog, but not when it's with a witness and certainly not in this circumstance. She reminds him of a couple he questioned during the Monroe murders. After questioning them Nate wanted to go home to soak.

"I have another statement from you, one that was taken the day before from another officer, in which you claim you had dinner with a girlfriend. Which statement explains your movements on the night in question?"

"Now why would I say that?" Her mouth pinches together. Eyes up to her left as if the answer is written among the cobwebs in the corner of the ceiling. "Well, I'm sure I was just confused."

"Did Mr. Whitehead ask you to cover for him that night?"

"I wouldn't do that." Now the eyes were wide, innocent.

"I'm not here to question your statement, or arrest you. I'm here to get information on Mr. Whitehead for a criminal investigation we're conducting right now."

"Now? Oh, I see." She looks to her left, finger on her bottom lip. "So if I tell you what I remember that night, I won't be incriminating myself?"

Nate shakes his head.

"I'll tell you that no good Charlie Whitehead." The words rush out of her as if she's been waiting a long time to tell them. "He promised me a hundred dollars to say that we went to dinner, and then came back to my place. I'd

145

been out with a friend of mine, Charlene, and when I came home he was waiting in the parking lot for me. He came up to my apartment and we talked. You could tell he was bothered by Ms. Fremont's death. He went home around two in the morning. Nothing happened, Detective Cliffton, he wasn't my type. Now you, on the other hand—"

"I don't mean to interrupt you Ms. Samples," Pete interjects and Nate is grateful. "You could really help us with an investigation. What time, exactly, did you arrive in your car park?"

She frowns for a minute. "You mean the parking lot? Around ten o'clock; yes, I'd say it was a few minutes before ten."

"And Charlie stayed until two?"

"Yes, we shared a bottle of wine and talked until then."

"Did he seem upset or agitated?" Pete asks.

"He's always twitchy." She waves a hand at them as if shooing off the idea. "He's better since the doctor put him on medication, but he'll always be acting as if everyone's out to get him."

"What kind of medication?" Nate asks, sitting forward on the pink settee, upsetting the pillows behind him.

"Honey, I'm not sure the name. Some brand that keeps a person with bipolar disorder calm I suppose. That's what he's got, you know. Bipolar Disorder. Had it since he was a kid."

Nate and Pete share a look.

"You said you haven't seen him in a couple years. Did you two have a falling out?" Pete asks.

146

Nate is taking notes.

"Oh, we saw each other now and then after that time I covered for him, but over the years we just drifted apart. Never did get my money."

"Thank you Ms. Samples. If we have any further questions may we call upon you?" Nate stands and tolerates another head-to-toe perusal.

"Honey, I'd be disappointed if I didn't hear from you again." She poses, pointing her right foot out to the side and behind her—old screen-goddess photo-op.

Nate and Pete retrace their steps to their car. Nate gets behind the wheel but doesn't put the key in the ignition, thinking. Pete glances over at him and asks, "Did you want to go back inside? I could come back, say in about an hour."

Nate shakes his upper body, "Not my type. Okay so far we've got two employees from PSA on medication, Richie Carson and Charlie Whitehead—"

"Don't forget there's a third employee, Kessler that Damone questioned."

"Yeah, but they had nothing on the guy other than Michelle went out on the boat he was piloting, but yeah, he's another we could have in for a little conversation. Also we should get Adamya in just for good measure. What boats are they usually assigned to?"

Pete flips through his notebook looking for the names of the boats and their crew that they'd gotten during their first visit to PSA. "Kessler captains *The Mosquito* and Carson usually crews it. Whitehead is assigned to *The Mariner*."

"Man I'd like to get inside those boats, get CSI in

147

with their lights." Nate thumbs the steering wheel. I wonder if we can weasel a warrant." He reaches into his jacket pocket for his cell phone. He connects to the DA's office and asks to speak to one of the junior attorneys, Jason Turnbull, a friend with benefits. Jason listens to the request and puts him on hold. Nate looks at Pete, "Whitehead feels right for it, but we can't tie him to it unless there's some secret hiding place where he keeps the ears."

"He could cannibalize them; he could put them in soup. Then there would be no way to tie him to the murders."

"You are a bit disturbing."

"So you think our killer keeps them on a boat?"

"That's what I'm hop—"

Jason comes back on the line. "Hey Hollywood. Can you tie all the victims to Puget Sound Adventures?"

"Yes and a missing person."

"And this man you are interested in, Charlie Whitehead, was also a suspect in a murder over two years ago?"

"Yes. It's a lot of coincidence I know, but it's all pointing to PSA. I've got to get on board their boats, just to rule them out you know."

"Word the warrant as if Charlie Whitehead is the only one you suspect at PSA, but that as far as you know he captains all of the vessels. That way we're not restricted to searching only one and mention his supposed medical history. I wish we could find out what that is and what medication he's on without a warrant," the attorney mutters.

"Thanks Jason, I owe you one."

"I'll remember that." Nate hangs up on the implied obligation.

**1:30 p.m.**

Pete finishes typing and hands Nate a printed copy of the warrant request to read before walking it to the DA's office. Nate looks at what is there. "It's a little skimpy. Oh well, I'll walk it over."

"Need company?"

"Nah, I'll get the warrant and be back here. Contact CSI to let them know we'll need them this afternoon."

Nate marches out of the office radiating confidence.

**3:30 p.m.**

After waiting, arguing, and pleading for two hours Nate leaves the DA's office empty-handed and Jason out of luck on a hook-up. He contacts Pete to let him know the warrant is delayed and wouldn't be in their hands until tomorrow and to hold off on CSI.

"I'll be there in a few. I want to drive over to the marina to bring in Adamya and Kessler."

**5:00 p.m.**

Richard Kessler sits at a table in the interrogation room looking at a bolt attached to a metal plate that is normally

149

used for hostile visitors. His eyes move from the metal ring to the mirror wall behind which Nate and Pete stand in the observation room watching him through the two-way glass. Kessler nods toward the mirror and smiles.

"Cheeky bastard." Pete says

"Let's see what he's been up to lately." Nate squares his shoulders and leads the way out one door and into the other. He smiles at Kessler and sits down opposite, Pete takes his position near the door. Nate arrived at the PSA office just after closing and Darius Adamya was nowhere to be found. Kessler walked in from the pier and Nate intercepted him on the way to his car with promises to bring him right back to it when they were done.

After greetings and the usual formalities were done, Nate says, "You know we had Richie in here awhile back?"

"Yeah, he told me. You scared him real good."

"We'd like to ask you some of the same questions," Nate reaches into his folder again bringing out several photos.

Captain Kessler takes the pile of photos into his hands like a deck of cards and starts dealing them out. "He looks familiar, what's his name?"

Kessler put the photo of Derek Southwell on the table and tapped it with his forefinger.

"Derek Southwell."

"Well, he looks like a guy who was aboard with a group; something a little different about the group, if you know what I mean."

Nate thinks he does know. "Which boat were you on?"

"*The Mosquito*, that's my boat."

150

"Who was crewing your boat the day this gentleman and his group went out?"

Kessler squints trying to remember. "Richie usually comes out with me. But something makes me think he wasn't out on that day." He shakes his head, "I can't remember. You should talk to Darius to see if he recorded it."

Nate nods, knowing Adamya is the person he wants to bring in next. The conversation went as follows: No he doesn't remember any of the others. No he's not sure he remembers what he was doing each and every night after work, but he can provide the name of his live-in girlfriend and the names of places he might go for a beer after work. No he's not on any type of medication besides the occasional aspirin. And no, no, no, he does not know who would want to harm anyone.

Nate finishes questioning the captain and gets hold of an officer to drive Kessler back to his car. Before Kessler leaves, he turns to Nate, "You should come out with me sometime, catch some fish."

Nate smiles out of the corner of his mouth, "Yeah, that's not going to happen."

Pete and Nate seem frozen in the empty hallway. Pete looks at Nate, "These people seem to have cut their own ear off before they chop their own head off and jump into Puget Sound. Has suicide been ruled out?"

Nate says to Pete, "I'm hungry."


**6:30 p.m.**

151

John and Susan face each other over half-finished plates of spaghetti. The dinner is winding down and they enjoy compatible conversation, a decent Merlot, and soft music from John's iPod. Before Susan arrived this evening, John ran around the apartment placing lavender-scented tea-lights in strategic spots, tossing items of clothing that he found on the floor into his bedroom closet, and straightening up books, record albums, and random piles of mail. The ambiance was worth the extra effort. Susan compliments the chef. "This was one of the most delicious meals I've ever eaten."

"One of the, not THE?"

"Well I know my way around a kitchen as well," she glances slyly at John.

This evening he learned about more similarities he had with Susan—she likes to go out in a light rain without an umbrella to look for rainbows, she's excited every time she sees a deer in the wild, and she saves her friends and family from imagined enemies in her dreams.

John impulsively stands and reaches for Susan's hand and they begin a slow dance to Chris Isaak's *Wicked Game*. John's eyes close and he puts himself into the moment. He enjoys the song, the scent Susan's wearing, and the feel of her in his arms. The song ends, John and Susan continuing dancing. John feeling as if he's in a warm dream-cocoon that he doesn't want to emerge from to become a moth that only wants to flutter against a bright light, but the cocoon dissolves when Susan stops and says, "Do it now."

John hesitates shaking off the gossamer threads of the cocoon, "Do what now?"

"Flashback."

Now the thing John has never done intentionally is flashback on, in, or near water, or while sitting in his third-floor apartment. There was just something about finding himself bobbing up and down surrounded by a lot of water with no boat in sight, or falling through the air because the apartment he's in used to be a single story building. He doesn't want to ruin the close feeling they've shared tonight, but is unsure how to explain his rules without seeming reticent about flashing back in front of her. His mouth opens to explain this and the doorbell rings. *Saved by the proverbial bell.*

He goes to the door, looks through the peephole, then opens the door to Nate and a man with styled brown hair and blue eyes. Nate walks right in, but the other man waits until John motions him into his apartment. It takes only a second to see Nate's face change when he sees Susan.

"I didn't think to call first. We've been working straight through since eight this morning and I smelled spaghetti sauce."

John cuts off his apology and assures them they should stay and asks if they can have a drink and points to the seating in the living room. "Join us. Nate, I want you to meet Susan. And you must be—" John reaches a hand toward Pete.

"Pete Cavanaugh." John's ears tickle as the foreign accent reaches them. John turns to Susan, "Honey, this is my friend Nate—Nate Cliffton, and this is his partner Pete Cavanaugh." Susan smiles her greeting and helps John clean the dining room table to clear a spot for them. Then

Susan serves up plates of spaghetti and John opens another bottle of wine. Nate provides a lively but brief update on the case at John's urging, then the conversation rolls around to rumors about the marijuana laws and complaints about the new police department oversight by the Mayor's office. In the middle of Nate telling the story of how Pete questioned Whitehead, Susan makes a noise—a brief, embarrassed bark, like a giggle at a funeral. Her face turns red. When John, Nate and Pete give her their full attention, she looks as if she's ready to laugh or cry. Finally she blurts out, "You're partners ... at work!" She nods as if encouraging them to participate. Nate and John realize what she's been thinking and Pete continues to smile at her, indulging her inane statement.

Nate looks at Pete and then at Susan, "He's too much of a neat-nik for me."

Pete continues to smile.

"So Pete, I can't help but notice your accent. What part of England are you from?" John quickly brings him back into the conversation.

"Yes, it is a bit of a giveaway. I'm from Wales, actually, Cardiff. This meal is delicious, by the way."

"Thank you. You're far from home. Do you miss it?"

"Of course, but I'm used to the weather you have here. Cardiff is similar to Seattle really. The city sits on the waterfront, and you cannot motor far before running into bluffs and hillsides. Although the weather is similar, I believe you see the sun a bit more here."

"Have you been to a Mariners game?" Pete shakes his head and John continues, "We've got to get you to a baseball game. Interested?"

"Brilliant, thank you for asking."

The guys plan a trip to Safeco Field later this summer, hoping that would give the detectives' time to close their case. Nate and Pete finish their meal and leave saying the two love birds should be able to finish their evening alone.

The door closes and John turns his attention to Susan who leans over and kisses him on the lips. John tastes the wine mixed with garlic from tonight's meal and warmth that is all Susan. He doesn't want the kiss to end, but it does.

"I kinda like your friends, John Carpenter."

John just wants to kiss her again so he says something he hopes will encourage another.

"I kinda like you, Susan Bishop."

It works.

## Chapter 26
### *June 18<sup>th</sup> – 9:30 a.m.*

John answers the phone, it is Nate.

"John what are you doing right now?"

Right now John is lying in bed, naked with a smile on his face and no intention of getting up. He's not even sure why he answered the phone.

"I'm a little busy right now, Nate." John leans over to kiss Susan who stayed the night after John tempted her with promises of his world-famous waffles for breakfast. She didn't hesitate, rather she called her father to let him know not to worry about her, turned the lights down and shimmied out of her little black dress. Then with a glance over her shoulders, led him into the bedroom where they stayed the rest of the night.

"Unbusy yourself, come to the marina with me." Nate reaches that special pitch in his voice that he usually only gets after he's used every other method to plead his case.

John is not moved. "Not going to happen this morning," and he lowers the phone from his ear and clicks End.

\*\*\*

"This afternoon then—" Nate says into the phone before realizing he's talking to air. Nate hangs up just as Kominski walks up to the companion desks of Nate and Pete.

"Got another witness who says she saw Crystal Knapp and Chuck Connors the night they disappeared."

Nate drags himself to attention, willing himself to care what Kominski or this witness will say. "Okay, bring her back, would ya."

Pete offers to make a fresh pot of coffee and Nate waves his hand, dismissing him. He stands and plasters a smile on his face when Kominski steps aside to allow a small woman of Asian heritage past him. Her black hair is touched with gray and pulled back into a bun. The crinkle lines at the outer edges of her eyes indicates she finds reasons to laugh. Her brown eyes are dark and quick, taking in Nate, the desk, and the space around him. She smiles and nods when Nate waves both hands toward the wooden chair, like a model showing the curtained prize or lighted letter. She gracefully settles onto the seat and smoothes a black skirt with her hands, absently pushing a lock of hair away from her eyes. Nate wishes he had a cushion to make her more comfortable. He sits and rolls his chair closer to Ms. Kumata. After getting through her name, occupation, if any, and contact information, Nate asks, "Tell me what you remember."

Ms. Kumata bites her lower lip, then nods to herself, as if she approves what she plans to say, "I own a gift shop next door to a saloon called The Trout Mouth. It was there that I saw the man and woman, the couple that were on the news, come out of the bar to the street. They were very drunk."

Pete walks up with a cup of coffee and an assortment of sugar in a square container and a creamer with liquid half-and-half. A spoon is placed near her and she looks up and smiles at Pete. Nate cannot help the rolling of his eyes, but snaps to attention when she looks

157

back at him. He smiles, encouraging her to go on.

"There was a man with them."

Nate is excited when she says this, but after several minutes of questions it becomes apparent that she did not see his face. "I only noticed him because of the unusual belt he wore. You see, I sell fine leather goods in my shop and his belt looked expensive."

"I take it the belt wasn't one from your shop."

"No. It was not one I recognized."

"Would you know of places that might sell something like the belt you saw?"

Ms. Kumata says she can give them some names. "The tooling on the leather, it was very intricate and looked like it was done by hand and I noticed a pouch sewn to the belt, like a holster."

"Holster? Did you see a gun?"

"No gun. I did not see what I thought was a gun, but I did see what I thought was a knife." She puts her hands in the air approximately ten inches apart. "Big one."


## 12:30 a.m.

John said goodbye to Susan at noon when she went to work. When she embraced him to say goodbye, she told him his look is endearing, but as he assesses himself in the mirror thoughts of Frankenstein's younger brother come to mind. His scalp is healing. Today his head looks like he fell asleep on a question-mark-shaped object, leaving a curvy impression on the right side—the red, angry scar turning pink tinged with purple. It tingles where the stitches are waiting to dissolve. Growing back asymmetric, his hair is short and downy on one side, thick and fly-away on the other. That's what he gets for adhering to doctor's orders of baby shampoo. *I look like a baby duck.*

Deciding he needs a burger fix, he leaves to stalk down the nearest drive-thru to quench his fast-food craving. Pulling his car past the squawk-box, he orders a burger and fries and a Coke and because Nate's phone call has him feeling guilty, he turns in the direction of the marina. Nate's been begging him to go there on the off-chance he has a useful flashback. John decides to drive to Shilshole, park the car, and have a picnic. He pulls into the parking lot and drives toward the Puget Sound Adventures sign in front of a shanty where, presumably, they do business. With the engine clicking as it cools, he pulls the fast-food paper bag onto his lap and munches a French fry.

"Food of the Gods," he mumbles aloud tasting the salt and oil goodness. He follows that mouthful with the taste combination of a somewhat questionable meat patty, cheese, ketchup, and pickle, finishing in three bites. Sipping on his fountain drink he watches the comings and goings of the workers and their fishing boats as several leave the marina for afternoon excursions. His eyes are on *The Mosquito*, still tied to the pier. It doesn't look like it's going anywhere. The bout of mild activity is over and quiet falls over the marina.

Scrunching the wrappers into one big ball and tossing them into the bag they came in, he reaches into the glove compartment for the binoculars he uses at sporting events and gets out of the car. He brings the field glasses to his eyes. The minute the lens are pressed against his eye sockets the scene changes to nighttime. The freaky flashback-curtain-rise startles him, but he keeps the binoculars to his eyes. *The Mosquito* sits quietly under the stars. The moon is full and John has no trouble making out the name of the boat, or the light-colored vehicle that pulls in and parks near it, just out of reach of the mounted outdoor light's circle. Holding his breath and pressing the eyepiece closer, fearful that the slightest change in position would interrupt the flashback, he watches a man get out of the vehicle and circle around to the trunk. There he bends to retrieve a blanket. He takes the blanket to the passenger side of the vehicle. John cautiously shuffles forward to get a clearer view.

*I should go.*

The man opens the passenger door and leans in. He fumbles around before he backs out with something in his arms. The something looks like a person wrapped in the blanket. John creeps a little closer.

*I should go, call Nate.*

An arm falls out of the blanket cocoon and swings in time with the man's gait. John gasps, only then realizing he is holding his breath. He watches the man walk to the boat undetected. As he passes beneath one of the few overhead lights on that stretch of dock, John sees the side of his face. There's no mistaking, this is the man he saw at the bar with Derek. High cheekbones. The way he carries himself. John's no longer moving forward.

*I should go, call Nate, and be safe.*

Although he knows his flashbacks will not cause him harm, that the scenes are like watching a movie film, he's still frightened by the bleak aspects of what he sees—

160

the dark, the man, and the arm. John's sure he could pick him out of a line-up. Time to call Nate, he's seen enough. He lowers the glasses hoping that will be enough to bring him out of the flashback and into real time. His triumph over returning to the sunny afternoon is short-lived as he comes face-to-face with high cheekbones and intense eyes—the man from the bar. The man he'd just seen carrying a body.

John's throat dries up and he forces words out of the arid windpipe, "Just staring at the boats," John tries for a nonchalant grin. "I just love boats."

A shadow flies toward his head causing John to duck and shift, putting his hands up. But that doesn't stop the object's arc, or the blow to the back of John's recently worked on skull. Darkness falls.


***


Nate's thinking about lunch until his phone rings. He picks up on the second chime. After saying Cliffton, he's silent until he hangs up and looks at Pete. "They won't do it. They won't sign a warrant without more evidence."

"What do you want to do?"

"I'm going over to PSA, see if Darius will come in and talk to us. Help us understand the workings of PSA and see if he's had any problems with any of the staff."

"You want me to come with you?"

"Nah, stay here and hold down the fort. I'll be back in a few."

"You're not going to do anything you shouldn't

161

without the warrant."

"Don't worry, Mum." Nate teases, using the affectionate British title.


## 1:00 p.m.

Pete sits at his desk on the phone. He's setting up a meeting with the bartender on duty the night Crystal and Chuck were in The Trout Mouth hoping the man Ms. Kumata saw with the couple left more of an impression—enough to pick him out of a book of mug shots. Pete's back is to the rest of the office so when Kominski comes up and starts talking he jumps.

"Hey Ianto, where's Captain Jack?"

"Excuse me?" Pete puts his hand over the mouthpiece.

"Torchwood? C'mon you're British and you don't know Torchwood?"

"I am well aware of Torchwood, but was confounded by your reference to Ianto when talking to me and, oh, bother, never mind."

"Well, where's Cliffton."

"He went to the marina. He should be back in a while."

Kominski shrugs as if he tried. Then he settles for talking with the hired help.

"Guy from IT was up here looking for you or Cliffton."

"When was this?"

"You guys were talking to Kumata. He dropped this

off. Said they cleaned up the picture from the surveillance camera and enlarged it as much as they could, used a new process."

Pete reaches for the flash drive and sticks it into his computer to see what IT came up with. He clicks around, looking for the file. As the file uploads and information begins to appear on his screen, he sits back with his phone cradled between his head and shoulder. He can smell the onions Kominski must have had for lunch or breakfast as the big man leans over to observe. Pete waits to see the face of Charlie Whitehead. He doesn't have to wait long before the picture is loaded and a close-up of the guy with their missing person Derek Southwell appears on the screen. Pete stiffens and slams the receiver of his phone onto the cradle.

"Detective Kominski, please tell Lieutenant Gale that we need cars at Shilshole marina. Officer in trouble. I'm heading there right now."

Pete gets out his cell phone and hits the speed dial button for Nate. The call goes straight to voicemail and Pete looks at his phone as if it were a disobedient child. He hollers at Kominski who turns eyes wide.

"And call Detective Cliffton. Tell him we've got the wrong guy."


*1:30 p.m.*

Nate rolls into the marina, sun baking the parking lot. As he nears the spots by Puget Sound Adventures office, he sees John's car. The car is empty. Nate looks around. Where would John be? He pulls out his cell phone and dials John's number. Nate knows John didn't go out fishing. *He likes being out on the water about as much as I do—never!* Nate climbs out of his own vehicle and realizes the ringing sound is in the air around him. His eyes focus on a Smartphone lying under the driver's side of John's car. When he picks it up, he sees his name displayed on the screen. Nate clicks off and the ringing stops to be replaced by alarms only he can hear, going off inside his head. Panic and guilt fight for supremacy—panic because his friend is missing outside of the PSA offices and guilt because it was him that kept insisting John get out here to test his flashbacks. Nate strides toward the office, hoping John's inside. The office-shack is locked and Nate walks around peering in every tiny window on two sides of the structure. Empty. Nate turns in a circle until he's pointed toward a docked boat, *The Mosquito*. It looks like no one's home there as well, but he starts toward it.

His shoes scatter gravel in the path leading to the pier. The sound echoes off of warehouses and water, reminding him of a deserted town with him the sheriff pacing toward the OK corral to face the enemy. No boat traffic, no sounds of fishing tackle, no fishermen telling tales, no movement in the parking lot. A chill runs up his back and settles in the hair at his neck. Tiny follicles spring to attention. Unclipping the holster holding his service revolver, he continues onto the pier with his hand lightly on the Smith & Wesson M&P.

"Ahoy," Nate yells, "Anybody home?"

He approaches the side of the boat, squinting into the sun, to see into the gloom of the interior. A shadowy figure comes out of the cabin. A cloud scoots in front of the sun.

"Oh, hey, Darius, I wonder if you can help me." Nate relaxes slightly, hand still resting on his gun and carefully climbs aboard. Darius carries a bucket in one hand filled with questionable liquid.

"Well, hello Detective. You surprised me. I was just getting ready to push off. Can this wait?"

"I wonder if you've seen a guy around here. Maybe he came to the office earlier, John Carpenter?"

"Name doesn't sound familiar, what's he look like."

"Dark hair, brown eyes, about this tall," Nate holds his hand near his shoulder. "His car's in the parking lot."

"Could be out on a charter. They won't be in until four."

"Can you check for me?"

"I've got to—"

"It's not a polite request, it's an order."

Darius' face transforms from customer-friendly to spoiled-surly. Isn't getting his way. Nate just smiles and stares at him, waiting for him to head in the direction of the office. In the silence, a moan drifts from the cabin. Darius' face makes another transformation from the surly look to sly and deadly.

"Darius, put down the pail. Put it down and put your hands out." Nate's gun is up and he attempts the proper stance on the gently rocking surface. The words are still echoing in the space between them when the pail flies toward his face. Nate's reaction is slow as his arm goes up to deflect the metal object. The edge of the pail hits his cheekbone spilling all the liquid inside down the front of

165

Nate's jacket. Chlorine hits his nostrils like a shot of smelling salts. Off-balance from the attack, Nate slips on the wet deck. Darius lunges toward him with a knife, slicing his upper arm. Before Darius can try again, Nate sees the blur as a white buoy arches toward the back of Darius' head, propelled by an unsteady John. Darius, startled, falls to his knees.

Nate scrambles to his feet. His Nunn Bush shoes slide around on the wet surface before the leather soles find purchase. He motions to John to move away and John goes to the side near the pier. Nate hears a police siren, then running thuds and Pete saying, *I've got your back"*

Nate points his gun at Darius. "You're under arrest. Stay down."

Darius rises to his feet. He straightens with a smirk on his face and the knife still in his hands.

"Put the knife down or I'll shoot."

Darius lifts an eyebrow.

Nate's gun is unwavering. Pete is behind him, yelling at Darius to put the knife down. Nate hears John, *You're bleeding Nate.*

Time stands still, his breathing, louder than all the other sounds. Nate watches Darius slowly spread his fingers letting the knife fall to the deck with a clatter. He doesn't bring his gun down. The pain in his upper arm starts to spread to his collarbone and down the forearm toward the wrist. The sight on his gun is pointed to a spot right between the blue eye and the hazel eye. He hears Pete.

*Nate, we've got him. Put your gun down.*

He should, right? He should put his gun back in its holster and arrest this guy. March him downtown. Read

166

him his rights. And if all goes well, Darius will never again see the outside of a jail cell. A conversation Nate had in May with Tom starts replaying in his head, as if someone pushed a switch. He wasn't thinking about it, it was just there. He listens to his past-self ask the question.

*"Thorazine, who would need that? What is it?"*

*"Used to treat some personality disorders. Excuse me, did I say treat?"* Tom cocks an eyebrow at Nate and shakes his head.

*"You did, I heard you."* Nate smiles back.

*"There is no treatment for personality disorder. Thorazine, or any other drug, is a waste of time. Just dopes them up. So drugged they're doing the Thorazine shuffle."* Tom at that point does a little jive shuffle across the floor.

*"That's harsh, Tom. I can't believe I just heard this from the nicest guy I know. Horrible dancer, nice guy."*

Tom gets serious. *"Between you and me, absence of life is the only treatment."*

The words echo.

A muscle in Nate's right arm twitches. His shoulders creak as he relaxes them, preparing to lower his arms. His eyes haven't left the other man's blue and hazel ones. Then in slow motion the lid over the blue eye slowly lowers—the wink, slow and seductive—while at the same time Darius' left hand slides behind his back. Nate doesn't remember fully depressing the trigger. Didn't feel the kick from the short recoil, or hear the bullet roar out of the polymer barrel on its way to the spot between the blue eye and the hazel eye. He becomes aware when he sees a bloom of red on Darius' forehead. Nate lowers the gun. Silence.

Like the cavalry, late to the massacre, two patrol

cars twist into the parking lot, tires throwing gravel, sirens blaring, and lights flashing. The spell is broken. Sound returns as if someone pushed the Mute button again to bring the noise back. Gunfire rings in his ears. Nate hears Pete asking John if he's all right.

*Just another bump on the head, good thing it's so thick.*

Pete waves to the cars. The officers arrive on the pier and Pete waves his badge, tells them that the man on the deck is Darius Adamya, a person responsible for the recent murders. He tells the officers to call an ambulance, but the four officers join the group and stare at the man crumpled at their feet.

*A hearse you mean. This guy's not going anywhere.*

Pete repeats the order, emphasizing officer injured. He walks up to Nate. "Darius Adamya is the person in the security photo with Derek Southwell outside of The Sea Unicorn. The picture came back from IT today."

Nate shakes off the numbness, looks at Pete and nods. Then he brings his hand up to the knife wound on the meaty part of his upper right arm and winches. Pete turns to one of the officers and asks if they have a first aid kit in their vehicle. Another officer asks what happened. Pete smoothly tells them the suspect wouldn't put the knife down. He was in a threatening position and holding a hostage. *Nate fired before I had a chance to.* Nate looks at Pete; then nods his head to confirm the story.

"You're hurt." Pete frowns.

"What, this? It's nothing." Nate winks and then turns to John and gives him a bear hug.

"You've ruined that lovely jacket Detective

168

Cliffton." John mumbles into the fabric.

"This? It's nothing." Nate releases him and turns back to Pete. He pulls him aside.

"Detective Cavanaugh." Nate coughs to clear his throat. "Pete, thank you."

## Chapter 27

*August 30*

"Well at least you only got stabbed once this time." John walks ahead of Nate and Pete.

"You're keeping track?" Nate absently touches his upper arm.

"Is this the queue?" Pete joins them in line for a beer.

John and Nate are taking Pete to an American baseball game. There were high hopes for The Mariners at the beginning of the season, but near the end the team had settled back into its less than .500 place. But the evening is the perfect temperature, baseball is normal and usually safe, and Pete's never been to one which should be good for a few laughs. Their seats are behind home plate; all three agreed that they would sit anywhere as long as they couldn't see Puget Sound.

"Bloody hell, will you two please be quiet. I would like to see you attend a rugby match and live to tell about it." Pete explodes after a few jibes.

"Oooo, rugby." John laughs, wiggling his fingers, and rolling his eyes.

"I've always wanted to go to a rugby match. All that muscle and sweat ..." Nate's rewarded with John's elbow in the ribs.

Nate and Pete bring John up-to-speed with the findings CSI had when they searched *The Mosquito*. John wrinkles his nose when he hears about the trophy box, a cigar box filled with several shriveled oblongs that vaguely resembled human ears, along with a bottle of Thorazine.

The blood match on the knives found in a leather pouch and the historical perspective provided by Darius' sister convinced authorities to close the case.

"There was a disposable cell phone on his body. IT said it was used once to a number of what must have been another disposable phone. Couldn't trace it."

"Does that bother you?" John asks his friend, trying to read his face.

Nate looks down at John, his mouth in a straight line. John watches the other man's blue eyes cloud, then clear, then cloud. "What's a working stiff like me going to do about it?"

John knows his friend is bothered by the loose end. There's nothing he can do right now to help him so he throws out a distraction and something he's been waiting to ask him. "I've got a special request for you. Be my best man."

Nate's mouth drops open. Then John is caught up in a bear hug where the words seem to rumble from Nate's chest rather than through the air. "You're seriously getting married?"

"I'm seriously getting married." John beams, face turning rose-colored. "I'm going to ask her soon. I haven't yet, I want to talk to her father first. But it will be soon. Maybe I'll propose around Christmas. That's romantic, right?"

"Congratulations buddy, I'm so happy for you." Nate says releasing John and Pete echoes the congratulations.

"It's a lot of responsibility. You have to promise you won't lose the ring. You'll be responsible for getting

171

me to the church on time. And no murders. No one can die before, during, or after the wedding."

"Geez, Mr. bossy-pants." Nate rewards John with a grimace.

"It's because the happy couple want everything to be perfect," Pete says to Nate.

"I promise; trust me, what could go wrong?" Nate boasts confidently.

Too bad John only has the ability to flashback instead of flash forward a year.

## Epilogue

The evening sun would soon be a memory. He stands on the bridge at the wheel of his pleasure cruiser. Tonight has been an exceptional night for trolling and his catch lies on the net in the stern of the forty-one foot boat. When the sun melts into the water he shuts down the engines and turns toward his catch.

She lay on her back, gagged with hands bound. He can hear a soft snuffle as she breathes. She'll be out a moment longer. He organizes his equipment. Raises the metal fillet table. When he turns to retrieve her, she's looking at him. Blue eyes slightly glazed as she shakes off the drug. It's show time.

He met her at a café this morning when they both stopped for coffee. She in running clothes, he in an expensive suit with cufflinks that cost more than her entire outfit plus three hundred dollars. A cup later they were chatting like long lost friends. She was headed back to Kansas in the morning. It didn't take much encouragement to agree to drinks that night, her last in town. Her last on Earth.

Grabbing her by the base of her pony tail he lifts her toward the fold out table. She screams and bucks trying to get away. But to where? The old swim or sex situation. Swim or kill. He jerks her head back and over the edge of the table, strangling another anemic scream. With one swift flick of the boning knife he cuts her throat, stiff-arming her away from him so the arterial blood sprays over the side of the boat. Her limbs twitch, her feet stutter in the air, and the gurgles come in spurts before quieting.

Time to feed the fish.

*No one to message about this one.*

He thinks about Darius. *Darius got careless.* Of course the police called him to tell him Darius was killed during an arrest for the murders of several visitors to the city of Seattle. He agreed to close shop for a while in cooperation with the police while they wrapped up their case. It won't set him back too much.

When he's done with the lady from Kansas he thinks about what he'll do when he gets back. *A nice meal at House of Prime Rib would be perfect right about now.*

However, before he heads back in. Before he disposes of this phone in his pocket. Before he morphs into another persona, another method of operation, one final message. His thumb hits the keys five times before hitting Send. He watches the bar steadily fill the top before flashing the message delivered confirmation, and then pulls his arm back and rockets forward, releasing the phone at the crest of the movement. It soars into the night. He listens for the splash. *More fish food.*

Willis Playford III weighs anchor, starts the engine, and heads home. In the air above him, the electronic characters in the message travel by radio waves to the control channel. They are redirected to cell phone towers. Arriving at the short message service center, the message will either be received by the phone it was sent or languish indefinitely.

*I win.*

*
**

Use the past to alter the future …

**Excerpt for Flashback To Baker Lake**

Read on for a look at Terri L.
Powers' terrifying third novel
starring John Carpenter and
Nate Cliffton

# Chapter 1
## Near Seattle, Washington

This moment in time, these precious few hours, a brief instant full of exquisite anticipation made more poignant by the days and weeks of planning and risk assessment are so quickly fleeting. Like sands of time, the hour trickles down to its final grains.

Lying near the boy, sheets tangled around my legs, I admire the smooth, sun-kissed skin of his shoulder; dipping to touch my nose against his flesh, inhaling the aroma of sweat and youth—a heady mixture that I never tire of. *I feel alive.*

The slender blonde is special. For a few hours we are lovers. I caress the boy's left shoulder, tracing a line down his back, sliding my hand over his buttocks, then back toward his right shoulder, following the curve in the small of his back, then down his right arm. I outline the purple and red marks that are beginning to show under the restraints at his wrists. My fingers continue to find new places they haven't been, watching the boy's eyelashes flutter against his cheeks, waiting. Cat and mouse. I know he's just pretending. I dip close and draw a circle on the tip of his ear lobe with my tongue. He jerks away.

A tight feeling in my stomach, an electric charge that jolts through my core, an arousal in my groin—naughty and exciting, so good because what I'm doing is so bad.

"It will be easier this time, Tommy. You'll see," I repeat the phrase I've been using since the night began. Leaning on my side, I slip on another condom, smearing lubrication on the tip. I balance over the spread-eagle youth—enter, thrust, *Oh God*—white lights explode in the brain as the boy's tightness swallows me, thrusting harder, finding my rhythm; his sobs only intensify the feeling. Too soon it's over and I collapse.

My breathing steadies. I rise and paddle barefoot to the bathroom, flushing the condom down the toilet and stepping into the shower. Fifteen minutes later I'm dressed and standing by the bed where the boy lies on sheets stained with proof he's no longer a virgin, hips raised, supported by two plump pillows placed under his mid-section, ankles secured like his wrists.

"You were delicious."

I ruffle the tousled hair before turning to leave. Down the stairway, out the front door of the hideaway in the forest, taking the wooden steps to the yard three at a time, and striding to the black Cadillac barely seen under the leafy canopy where timid moonlight ventures thinly. I climb in. The car slowly backs around and rolls up the driveway to the quiet road where it turns in the direction of Cascade Highway, a lone vehicle on a three-hour trip home.

"The police radio mentioned a tie-up near town that may cause a delay." The driver informs me.

"Well, if that don't white wash the chickens. Do the best you can."

"A pleasant evening, Sir?" the driver's eyes catch mine in the rearview mirror.

"It was, Joey. Thank you."

**Chapter 2**
**August 1 – 8:00 a.m.**
**129 Days Before the Wedding**

"John? What team lost Super Bowl fourteen?"

Susan is lying in bed with her knees up, a crossword propped across them, and three pillows behind her back, chewing on the end of the pencil she holds in her left hand, a slight frown on her lovely face, her hair a mussed halo.

"Mmmpfh?"

John is lying on his stomach, the covers up to his shoulders, and one pillow over his head as if he is Punxsutawney Phil burrowing to avoid his shadow.

"You must know this; you watch football every waking hour in the winter and I can't finish my puzzle without the answer." She pokes him.

"I know the Seahawks won Super Bowl forty-eight. I wasn't even born for fourteen; Google it."

"I can't Google it; that would be cheating."

John comes out from under the pillow, his dark-brown hair sticking up in all directions.

"Well someone put a lot of time and effort into gathering all of that information and putting it into a search engine so that you could find it, so I think you should put it to good use. Don't think of it as cheating, think of it as efficient. Now let me sleep."

"You can't honey, remember we are meeting with the caterers at ten. We have to go over menus for the reception and come to some kind of agreement – somewhere between hot dogs and beer, and prime rib and champagne."

"I like hot dogs and beer." John is teasing her. His composure covers the fact that he's really a happy, excited, romantic fool who can't wait to step down the aisle.

"I know sweetie, so do I, but I'm not spilling mustard on the front of a gown I just paid four installments for."

The planning has been going on for nine months, right after John asked Susan's father for her hand. This part of the process is nothing compared to sitting across from Steven at the Bishop home. That was intense. Susan had left them alone in the study to talk and get to know one another without her hovering. After chatting about the weather and the Seahawks chances, John stammered, *Mr. Bishop. I want to ask you for your blessing to marry your daughter.* The silence after this outburst seemed to stretch on for hours. Finally Steven spared him any more embarrassment by giving his well wishes and quieting John's apologies for the outburst by holding his hand up and saying, *Sometimes we say what we plan to say with our brain, and sometimes our heart takes over and says what it must, and the brain has to take a back seat.* John will never forget that statement because it seemed so appropriate at the time.

Today John can see the light at the end of the wedding planning tunnel. Susan asked John's sister, Brandy, to be her maid of honor. John is having his friend, Nate Cliffton, stand up with him. The wedding is scheduled for mid-December so John's goal is to stay out of Susan's way, help where he can, say yes as much as possible, and smile. Always smile.

"Hey, maybe we could visit the site of Super Bowl XIV and you could flashback to see the player's uniforms."

Susan's referring to the little ability John picked up while lying in a hospital in a coma a couple of years back after a near-fatal car crash. Now he can slip into the past. Not interact with it, merely watch. *Yesterday, the today of the past.* It's gotten him into a little trouble, but he's been a hero as well.

"Oh, that sounds like a productive use of our weekend." He rolls over and throws his arm over Susan's mid-section, covering the puzzle and pulling her towards him. "How about instead of solving a crossword puzzle, we play doctor?"

Susan giggles. "John, what about the caterers?"

"We've got time for one exam, Nurse Bishop," and he nuzzles the side of her neck.


**8:15 a.m.**


Nate Cliffton's sitting at his desk, barely hiding the fact that he's waiting. Waiting for Detective Pete Cavanaugh who usually arrives at this time with a cappuccino in one hand and a bag of biscotti in the other, all for Nate—one of the things that endears the detective to him. Nate and Pete have been partners for a little over a year, since the Puget Sound murders. And even though Nate's had to give up being the lone wolf, Pete's charm and the biscotti treat have won him over.

Nate again picks up yesterday's paper to continue the crossword puzzle he's doing, trying to think of a six-letter word for brusque. Captain Bishop brings him to attention by slamming his fist on his desk. Nate jumps in his chair.

"Not doing anything I see, I want you to work on a case out of GACS. A child abduction gone wrong. It's a murder case now."

Nate recovers his composure. "GACS taking lead?" GACS stands for the Gender and Age Crimes section that is responsible for the sexual assault and child abuse unit. The unit investigates sex crimes and child kidnappings.

"No, I want you on it. They don't usually handle homicide. But you'll be working with their man, Sergeant Quentin Parks. Think of it as community—they need our help, we're helping family."

Nate nods and asks, "Hey Captain, tell me something. Are you in the running for Chief? I'm just curious cuz I heard something about it. Good luck to you if you are."

"Don't start brown-nosing now, you might mess up your coiffure," Bishop winks and walks away leaving Nate to contact the guy in GACS.

"Parks." A deep growl on the other end of the call. Nate pictures a massive ex-defenseman with tattoos on his knuckles and a perpetual scowl. If Nate were a more timid soul he may have been tempted to end the call before it began.

"Sergeant Parks, this is Detective Nate Cliffton with Homicide. I was asked to call you about a case. Can we get together today to go over the details of the investigation?

"That is really considerate of you Detective. I am in need of someone who will bring me my coffee, take my

182

clothes to the dry cleaners, and fetch the paper for me. When can you begin?"

The sarcasm throws Nate off his guard. It takes him a second to recover. "Well, you can begin by not being such a wiseass and I'll begin by coming to your office at one. How is that for a start?"

"Look, how about if I just update you with emails as the investigation goes along and you report to your boss that we are working together and everyone will be happy."

The guy doesn't seem to want his help, but Nate charges forward. "One o'clock it is then."

"I can hardly wait."

Nate clicks his cell phone off and shakes his head. He didn't like working with other units or agencies. *Okay, as a rule I don't like working with others, usually.* Nate's been dating a guy from the U.S. Coast Guard so his rule can be broken.

Nate looks up as Detective Pete Cavanaugh walks up to their grouping of desks. Pete has Nate's cappuccino and biscotti, his own morning beverage, a newspaper, some file folders, and a novel with a bookmark sticking out of the end of it balanced in his two hands.

"Good day." The Welsh vowels make the two words sound like four. Pete sits down to face him at the desk opposite. "Morning paper," he raises his eyebrows and holds today's paper across the two desk tops for Nate's perusal. His accent softens the words and makes it sound as if he's singing a little ditty. Nate loves the way words sound when they come out of Pete's mouth, but he'll never let on to the cocky Englishman because that would give him too much leverage.

"Cool," Nate smiles and grabs for the paper as he settles in with his coffee and baked treat. "By the way, we've got a case."

"Murder?"

"Yep. Kidnapping first. Then it segued into murder."

"Hmm?"

"The Captain wants us to take the lead, work with GACS. We have a meeting with Sergeant Quentin Parks at one o'clock. Hopefully the asshole keeps the appointment."

"Are you making friends and influencing people already this morning." The innocent expression on Pete's face belies the sarcastic question.

"It's my specialty," Nate smirks.


**1:00 p.m.**

Nate and Pete arrive at the front desk in GACS and ask for Sergeant Parks.

"Won't you have a seat, I'll let him know you are here," the receptionist, a uniform officer, told them.

"We can just find him if you point us in the right direction." Nate bristles at having to wait.

The bespeckled redhead apologizes, but insists they wait. Nate looks pointedly at the clock above her head and back down at her, before producing a model-perfect smile and sitting down. At one-twenty Nate turns to Pete, "Let's go. I don't really want—"

"Detectives Cliffton and Cavanaugh?" The gravelly voice booms around the waiting area, seeming to bounce

184

off the walls and furniture. Nate jumps. He turns to face the man and notices two things. The first is the glint of satisfaction in the man's eyes that he got a rise out of Nate, and the second, Parks is only five-six with a willowy build. *Where does that voice come from?* Nate holds out his hand by way of introduction and nods. "This is my partner Detective Cavanaugh."

"Pleased to meet you sir." Pete murmurs.

"Wales?" Parks asks, ignoring Nate's hand and putting his hand out to Pete.

"Why yes, Cardiff to be exact." Pete shakes the proffered hand.

"I studied there when I was in college. I'll never forget the dialect. Follow me."

Nate puts his hand down, allowing Pete to precede him as they follow Parks to his desk in the right angle wing of the room.

"Sit down, sit down," Parks indicates the chairs facing his desk. "You are here to help me on the child abduction cases."

"Cases?" Nate hesitates. "It was my understanding this was a recent abduction that resulted in murder and we were to take the lead."

"Tommy Hull is the boy who was found dead. The FBI are interested, of course, they are looking into sex trafficking of minors, transporting them across borders. I'm very interested because this is the eighth boy that we know of to disappear from this northern area in the past few years.

"Any DNA evidence collected?" Pete asks.

"Nothing substantial; some samples collected where the body was dumped, but nothing that we can use to find the killer. We did get a match with another one of our case on the tire imprints found at the scene, but there is nothing unique about the tire—manufactured here in the United States, sold by dealers nationwide, one hundred and twenty dealers and repair shops here in Seattle proper."

"And you were treating the murdered boy as one of a series of abductions because of the tire mold. Where's Tommy's body?" Nate looks down at the open file and a picture of a blonde-haired boy with big brown eyes and an impish smile. He looks to be around eight or nine, the face still soft and round with youth.

"It went to King County. I've got the report here; cause of death was drug overdose."

"And you're sure it's not just an accident?"

"I'll send you a copy of the file on the Hull boy. Preliminary autopsy indicates there were ligature marks around the ankles and wrists and he was sexually assaulted, nothing consensual about those wounds. And there's nothing accidental about having too much chloral hydrate in his system. Like it or not boys, I'm very much involved."


**2:00 p.m.**


Mumford Edward Hurlburton III, Eddie to his constituents, at fifty-one is the youngest in the field of Republican candidates considering the run for Presidency. Currently a U.S. Congressman, he stands for baseball, apple pie, and the American way of life. Eddie's good looks and forward-

186

thinking mind—using social media to steer voters toward his issues, skills that others in his party lack—will propel him to the front. With chemically-enhanced brown hair, crinkles at the outer corners of his brown eyes, trim body, and six-five frame, he can pass for almost half his age. And his secret weapon, a smile that will brighten any billboard. Married to Molly for thirty years, with two daughters, Lynette, 14, and Matilda, 8, he is an exemplary example of what America would look like if everyone went to church, believed in the Lord, and followed the Hurlburton's example of Christian living. Amen brothers and sisters.

Molly is vying for the White House, ever since her husband was an up and coming attorney with powerful friends. She dresses the part and delivers her lines as well as any Oscar winner in Hollywood. Striking her given name, Mildred—a name that puts lunch lady shoes and a hairnet in the hearts and minds of voters—taking a name more benefitting a respectful First Lady. "Mildred is such a spinster schoolmarm's name." She says whenever anyone forgets and calls her by her given name. "Please call me Molly." Both girls were groomed for the spotlight from an early age, either as contestants in beauty contests, or as members of Science Olympiad and school forensics clubs. They each know two languages—Lynette, Spanish and French; Matilda, German and Japanese—and both are in ballet, swimming, creative writing, and horseback riding.

Today Eddie is headed to the offices of one of his biggest financial backers, Desmond Gravosso. He knows today's meeting could turn the tide in the direction that is needed for his upward climb if he is willing to back the deal that Gravosso wants. It would mean bending a little and pushing some things aside.

"Sir, Mr. Gravosso's son, Tristano, is playing soccer now and his team won the division trophy this past weekend." Evan Powell, campaign manager/aide/right-hand man/friend briefs Eddie.

"Tristano, huh, pretty good soccer player?

"Got the winning goal; he was voted team captain second year in a row."

"Thank you, Evan, I'll remember that."

As they pull up in front of the Gravosso office building, Eddie asks Evan "Is there a proposal on the table to help Gravosso with his project that won't make it look like I caved into greed?"

"There is a way to get around it if we piggyback the proposal onto the Republican economic bill that is going through the House right now. Make it look like it would be good for sustainability a way to build for the future."

"Well, if that don't whitewash the chickens. I like it, let's go with that. Make sure I'm meeting with the Representative supporting the bill before the week is up."

**About the Author:**

Terri L. Powers is the creator of the Flashback series that includes Flashback To The Dragon and Flashback To The Mosquito, with a new book coming out soon, Flashback To Baker Lake. A novice, she has filled many hours of her life reading—a library or book store are two of her favorite places to be.

Terri lives in Michigan with her husband and their one child. A retired State government manager, Terri focuses on writing her next novel.

www.ingramcontent.com/pod-product-compliance
Lightning Source LLC
Chambersburg PA
CBHW060809120626
46557CB00001B/145